SCHELMUFFSKY

# UNIVERSITY OF NORTH CAROLINA
## STUDIES IN THE GERMANIC LANGUAGES
## AND LITERATURES

NUMBER THIRTY-THREE


UNIVERSITY
OF NORTH CAROLINA
STUDIES IN
THE GERMANIC LANGUAGES
AND LITERATURES

Christian Reuter's

# Schelmuffsky

Introduction and English Translation

by

Wayne Wonderley

AMS PRESS INC.
New York
1966

*Manufactured in the United States of America*

# INTRODUCTION

What is Schelmuffsky? From the point of view of the historian of literature this tale fits rather conveniently into the genre of the novel of satire, specifically, satire of the picaresque novel and the novel of travel or phantasy. Both types essentially are predicated upon adventure. The Renaissance had imparted a new impetus to satire. A mere enumeration of one outstanding literary contribution from four Western European lands may suffice to point this up: Cervantes' *Don Quixote* (1605f, German translation 1621f); Erasmus' *Praise of Folly* (*Moriae encomium* 1509, German translation 1534); More's *Utopia* (1516, German translation 1524); Rabelais' *Gargantua et Pantagruel* (1532f, German translation 1575). Stimulated by continuing voyages of discovery, the seventeenth century European was fascinated by exploits or phantasies of travel and adventure. Perhaps the phenomena of atomic development and interest in the exploration of space are comparable modern reactions. The historical perspective may be focused more sharply if one remembers a few important authors and titles. Either leading up to or extending somewhat beyond 1700 (the dates of publication for *Schelmuffsky* are 1696-1697) one should recall that *Lazarillo de Tormes* (about 1554, possibly by Mendoza), translated from Spanish into various languages, including German in 1614, set the pace for the picaresque style of novel and fathered many imitations from Thomas Nash's *The Unfortunate Traveller* (1594) through Defoe's *Moll Flanders* (1722). *Gil Blas* (1715-1735) by Lesage is the most influential representative of the happy-go-lucky vagabond in French literature. The most famous novel of the German seventeenth century, Grimmelshausen's *Simplicissimus* (1688), certainly evidences picaresque influence. Centuries before, around 1200, Wolfram von Eschenbach's *Parzival*, had emerged as the type of naive, blundering simpleton who in spite of his apparent dullness seems to fare rather shrewdly and well. *Simplicissimus* continues this tradition. It is quite understandable that the phantastically adventurous imitators of *Simplicissimus* overshot their mark and thus practically invited parody.

Of course, there were other types of novels whose bombastic excesses in style and content Reuter wanted to lampoon, for example, the boorishness of Johann Fischart's Rabelaisian *Gargantua* (1575). Beginning in 1569, translations and variations of the romance *Amadis* tales and related prolix novels of the heroic-galant genre (for instance, Barclay's *Argenis* 1621, German translation 1626-1630) began to inundate the German reading public. (Cervantes' *Don Quixote* was a model in the fight against the *Amadis* type). Incidentally, one of Reuter's chief weapons directed against the various types of turgid novels which he is burlesquing is platitudinous detail. It seems that polemics must be exaggerated to be effective. In addition to some direct thrusts at the heroic-galant novel, *Schelmuffsky* appears also to take a few side strokes at the pastoral (for example, Sidney's *Arcadia* 1590, German translation 1629). It is noteworthy that important elements of the simpleton, travel, adventure, and utopian categories were soon to coalesce in Defoe's renowned *Robinson Crusoe* (1719) and touch off a whole series of German Robinsons, the most substantial representative being Schnabel's *Insel Felsenburg* (1731-1743).

We have at best only a scanty record of Reuter's life. The salient facts may be related briefly. Christian Reuter was born in 1665 near Halle of peasant stock. We know nothing of his boyhood. In 1688 Reuter was attracted to Leipzig to study theology. However, he decided rather soon that the study of law was perhaps more to his taste. In any case he apparently participated wholeheartedly in colorful student activities, including required drinking and folksy rowdyism.

In 1694 Reuter took up quarters at the "Red Lion" in Leipzig. The proprietress, who liked to affect airs of nobility, was the widow Müller who also brewed and dispensed a good "sticky beer" and who had a good-for-nothing son (Schelmuffsky's prototype) and two teenaged daughters. However, we are given to understand that all three women were unattractive and stupid, yet coquettish. Trouble developed when the widow refused to extend additional credit to Reuter and turned him out. Greatly piqued, Reuter gave vent to his feelings in 1695 by dashing off a satiric comedy (*Die ehrliche Frau zu Plissine*) lampooning the Müller family with only a thinly veiled disguise. Touches à la *Molière* directed against pomposity and preciosity are unmistakable. A sequel (*Der ehrlichen Frau Schlampampe Krankheit und Tod*) followed in 1696. These satires caught on in the city and the widow Müller found herself and family the targets of general derision. It was more than she could stand. She sought legal redress against Reuter. Sentences were handed down, fifteen weeks' imprisonment and expulsion for two years from the university for Reuter. He was also temporarily forbidden to leave Leipzig in case he should be summoned again, and was admonished to refrain from further personal satires. Of course, Reuter ignored these stipulations and proceeded to write in 1696 the first version of *Schelmuffsky*, presumably after a visit near Hamburg. A second version, the text of the present translation, appeared in the winter of 1696-1697. Expanding and polishing, Reuter converted the original version into two parts, at the same time promising a third part which never materialized. Traces of the feud with the Müllers remain, although on the whole the new version smacks considerably less of personal vengeance and is generally drawn in broader outline. Concerning the rest of Reuter's life we know little more than that he was in Dresden in 1697 and later in Berlin, continuing his literary production. He died about 1712.

Who is Schelmuffsky, the "hero" of this capital tale? He is at once a Gargantua, Don Quixote, Falstaff, Don Juan, and a Münchhausen. He is a naive, egocentric, bourgeois simpleton with delusions of aristocratic grandeur. The devil take him, who may challenge his preemptive prowess? Whom has *Fortuna* more favored than him with his marvelous birth and his astounding precociousness? Who can turn a phrase more politely or present a more gracious *compliment?* Whom do the ladies throw themselves at? Who is quicker or more adept with the sword than he? Who can imbibe more, who has been farther abroad—in short, to whom is more honor due?

At a first perusal of *Schelmuffsky* the modern reader is struck not only by the self-important deportment and attitude of Schelmuffsky but also by the contrasting pomposity and folksiness of the language and style. Of course there are fashions in language which change in accordance with laws comparable to those governing styles in women's clothes. Shakespeare for example does not speak the same English as we. In general the seventeenth century sentence is longer and heavier than what we are used to today. (For increased clarity and convenience, the present translation reduces the original length of some sentences without sacrificing accuracy. The translation aims primarily at fidelity and, it is hoped, felicity, while at the same time preserving a number of "quaint" linguistic or typographic features in order to suggest the yesteryear flavor of the book). No reader will fail to notice the recurrence of stock phrases, one purpose of which, as with Dickens, is to create a ludicrous effect. Among other noteworthy devices exaggeration, redundancy, and a somewhat drastic dose of Rabelaisian earthiness may be mentioned. Finally, we should bear in mind the two-pronged nature of humor involved in this tale. It is not only inherently humorous, but, to the seventeenth century reader, it was a gelogenic satire of novelistic flatulence. It may thus be regarded justifiably as a "novel of manners", because it ridicules the aspirations of the bourgeois to keep company with aristocrats. At the same time *Schelmuffsky* is an unconventional social satire presenting illuminating glimpses of the mores and mentality of its time. Superficially it is, in essence, a fabrication composed by its author tongue-in-cheek. This fact does not preclude the possibilities of profound analysis. As in *Don Quixote* or *Huckleberry Finn*, there can be various interpretive approaches. Thus, whether *Schelmuffsky* is to be regarded exclusively as persiflage and entertainment or, in a deeper sense, as an expression of baroque pessimism, are matters best left to the judgment of each reader. *Quantum vis* and *De gustibus non est disputandum.*

In any case, as long as the urge to laugh and banter is part and parcel of being a human, just so long will the attraction of *Schelmuffsky* last. Because this rollicking, frolicking novel has now stood the test of some two hundred and sixty years, it is reasonable to assume that its appeal will be lasting.

# Schelmuffskys

### Warhafftige
### Curiöse und sehr gefährliche

# Reisebeschreibung

### Zu

# Wasser und Lande

### I. Theil/
### Und zwar
### die allervollkomenste und accurateste
## EDITION,
### in Hochteutscher Frau Mutter Sprache
### eigenhändig und sehr artig an den
### Tag gegeben
### von
## E. S.

## Gedruckt zu Schelmerode/
### Im Jahr 1696.

# Schelmuffsky's

Veritable

Curious and Very Dangerous

# Travel Account

by

# Sea and Land

## First Part

Being

the most complete and most accurate

## Edition

published in our High German Mother Tongue

personally and very nicely

by

# E. S.

Printed at Schelmerode

in the year 1696

TO

The Right Honorable

GREAT MOGUL/

The Elder/

/world renowned King

or rather

Emperor of India

at Agra/ etc., etc.,

My sometime Lord

who was most friendly

on my very dangerous trip / etc.

Right Honorable
Potentate, etc.

I should be, the devil take me, a right ungrateful fellow if I were not concerned how to recompense the benefaction of Your Right Honorable Magnificence which I enjoyed recently on my very dangerous trip full fourteen days long; well, I should have done just this long ago if I had oniy known wherein I should have been able to tender Your Right Honorable Magnificence a favor. To be sure at first I was of a will to send along for this purpose to Your Grace and Dearest Spouse a keg of good sticky beer from our land; however I feared that the long way thither might make it weak and sour and that consequently you might not be able to drink it; in the meantime accordingly I left it cn route.

However since I have fetched forth and published my veritable, curious, and very dangerous travel account by sea and land, I have not been able to withstand the temptation (especially because I know that Your Grace and Right Honorable Magnificence is an especial connoisseur of curious books and novelties and because I promised you to send a book from Germany to India by way of return for your money and kind words) ; I hit upon the idea of dedicating my curious and very dangerous travel account to you and of sending along a copy bound in pigskin; I don't expect, the devil take me, a farthing for this, even though it is something curious, I only want the **Right Honorable Potentate** to see that I am grateful, and I hope it will please the Same. To be sure I don't want to brag a lot about this; however, the work will, the devil take me, praise the master himself, and when you have read through it may I request that Your Grace and Right Honorable Magnificence may also want to let Your Dearest Spouse read it so that she too may see what a fine fellow I was and how finally things went so unfortunately for me on the Spanish Sea. For the rest may Your Grace think the best of me and fare well, for this I remain

for your Right Honorable Magnificence
as well as for
Your Dearest Lady
forever
your most obliging,
most travel-ready
Schelmuffsky.

## To The Curious Reader.

I am, the devil take me, a real procrastinator that I have held back so long my veritable, curious, and very dangerous travel account on sea and land and have not long since published that which I had completed a considerable time ago. Why? The devil take me, many a person has hardly heard a city or country mentioned before he sits down immediately and indites a travel account ten yards long; when you read such stuff (especially someone like me who has traveled boldly) you can see right away that he has never stepped outside the door of his room, not to mention the fact that his nose is supposed to have smelled foreign and nasty winds like me. I may well admit, even though I've been around so many years in Sweden, so many years in Holland, so many years in England, also fourteen whole days in India with the Great Mogul, and elsewhere far and wide in the whole world, have seen, experienced, and gone through so much, nevertheless, should I recount all such things, your ears would pain you. But my lifelong I never did any bragging or boasting about this aside from the fact that occasionally I told of it to good friends on the beer bench. However in order that the world may hear and learn that I didn't always sit behind the stove and nibble my Mother's baked apples from the roaster, I do want to publish of my often very dangerous travels and chivalrous deeds by sea and land, as also of my imprisonment at St. Malo, such an account the like of which has never yet been found in a public print, and of which those who in time may desire to see foreign countries may make excellent use. However should I know that that which I have written down with great effort and diligence might not be believed by everyone, it would, the devil take me, pain me sorely that I had spoiled some quills thereby; but I hope the curious reader will not be superstitious and take this my very dangerous travel account for mere bragging lies, because, zounds, everything is true and, the devil take me, not a single word made up; for the rest I shall like to hear people say: My lifelong I've never read such a travel account; if this happens, then let everyone be assured that in time I shall not only fetch forth the second part of my veritable, curious, and very dangerous travel account by sea and land of oriental countries and cities, as well as of Italy and Poland, but my lifelong I shall also call myself,

> the curious reader's
> always
> most travel-ready
> Schelmuffsky.

## The First Chapter

Germany is my fatherland, I was born in Schelmerode, at
St. Malo I was a prisoner for a whole half year, and I was also
in Holland and England. However in order that I arrange this
my very dangerous travel account in a nice, orderly manner I
suppose I should begin with my marvelous birth: When the big
rat which had eaten my Mother's quite new silk dress could not
be killed with the broom as it ran between my sister's legs and
unexpectedly got into a hole, the worthy lady falls on this account from exertion into such an illness and faint that she lies
there for full twenty-four days and can, the devil take me, neither
move nor turn. I, who at that time had never yet seen the world
and who according to Adam Riese's arithmetic book should have
been waiting concealed four full months still, became so foolish
on account of the cursed rat that I could no longer remain concealed, but looked where the carpenter had left the hole and
quickly crawled out to daylight on all fours. Once born, I lay
eight full days down at my Mother's feet in the bed straw before
I could rightly realize where I was. The ninth day I looked at the
world with great astonishment, zounds! How barren everything
appeared to me, I was very sick, had nothing on, my Mother had
stretched out all four and lay there as if she had been struck on
the head; I didn't want to cry either because I lay there like a
young piglet and didn't want anyone to see me because I was
naked, thus I didn't know what to do. I was also of a will to wander back into concealment, but, the devil take me, I couldn't find
the way again whence I had come.

Finally I thought, you must really see whether you can cheer
up your Mother and I tried this by various ways and means;
first I took hold of her nose, next I tickled the soles of her feet,
now I patted her a little, again I then plucked a hair here and
there, again I touched a wart on her breast, but she wouldn't
waken from this; finally I took a straw and tickled her left nos-
tril at which she started up hastily and cried: "A rat! A rat!"
Upon hearing her say the word rat I felt, the devil take me, exactly as if someone took scissors and were cutting out my tongue,
whereupon I forthwith began to utter a terrifying ouch! My
Mother previously had cried out "A rat! A rat!" now she must
have shrieked "A rat! A rat!" over a hundred times, for she was

convinced that a rat was nestling down at her feet. However I was quick to crawl up to my Mother very nicely, looked up to her over the cover and said: "Mother, fear not, I'm no rat, but your dear son; but it's a rat's fault that I appeared so prematurely." Zounds! How happy was my Mother when she heard this, that I had been born so unexpectedly that she hadn't known anything of it at all. I just won't tell anyone how she, the devil take me, hugged and kissed me. After she had thus fondled me in her arms a good while, she got up with me, put a white shirt on me, and called in the renters from the whole house who all looked at me most astonished and didn't know what they should make of me because I could chat so nicely already.

Mr. George, my Mother's tutor at the time, thought that I was possessed of the evil spirit, otherwise things couldn't possibly be right with me, and he wanted to exorcise the same from me. Thereupon he ran immediately to his study and appeared hugging a big book under his arm with which he intended to exorcise the same from me. He chalked a big circle in the room, wrote a lot of gibberish letters within the circle, made the sign of the cross before and behind him, then stepped into the circle and began to intone the following:

> Hocus pocus black and white,
> Leave forthwith as I indite
> Schuri muri the little fellow;
> Since Mr. George so does bellow.

After Mr. George had spoken these words, I began to speak to him: "My dear tutor, why do you attempt such nonsense and think I am possessed of the evil spirit; if you only knew why I learned to speak so fast and why I was born so prematurely you certainly would not have attempted such a foolish business with your hocus pocus. Zounds! When they heard me speak thus, how astonished the people in the house were. Mr. George stood there in his circle, the devil take me, so shaking and trembling that everybody around could perceive from the air that the tutor evidently was not in any garden of roses.

But I couldn't stand his pitiful condition any longer and began to relate my astonishing birth and how it was due solely to that rat which had eaten the silk dress that I had arrived so prematurely and could talk so soon. Now after I had told everyone in the house circumstantially the entire incident about the rat

they finally believed that I was my Mother's son. But Mr. George
was ashamed as a dog for trying such silly tricks on my account
and believing that an evil spirit must be speaking in me. He was
quick to erase his hocus pocus circle, take his book and walk out
of the room silently with his damp and foul-smelling breeches.
How then everybody acted, hugging and fondling me, because I
was such a beautiful boy and could chat with them right away,
that would beggar description, the devil-take me, indeed they all
insisted right away that the very day amidst a crowd of people I
should receive the excellent name of Schelmuffsky. The tenth
day after my astonishing birth I gradually learned, although
somewhat slowly, to walk by benches, for I was quite sick for
neither having eaten nor drunk because Mother's teat was too
distasteful to me and I couldn't get used to any other food yet,
so that, if it hadn't turned out this way, I should probably have
had to die for lack of food and drink. What happened? That very
day my Mother had placed a big tub full of goat's milk on the
stove bench which I come upon by chance, dunk my finger in
it, taste, and because the stuff tasted very good I seized the whole
tub and, the devil take me, drank it all down, after which I became quite lively and strong. When my Mother saw that goat's
milk agreed with me, she was quick to buy another goat, for she
already had one, and so they had to nourish and rear me with
nothing but this stuff up to my twelfth year. I may say that the
day I turned twelve I had, the devil take me, several yards of
bacon on my back, for I had got so fat from the goat's milk. With
the beginning of my thirteenth year I likewise learned to nibble
down quite gently roasted stuffed birdies and larded young poultry, which eventually also agreed with me very much. As I was
now growing older my Mother sent me to school, thinking she
would now make a lad of me, who in time would exceed everyone
in scholarship; indeed at that time I should probably have become something eventually if I had had any desire to learn, but
I came out of school just as bright as I went in. My greatest
pleasure was the pea-shooter which my Grandmother had presented me from the fair at the Ass Mead; as soon as I came home
from school I threw my little books under the bench and took my
pea-shooter, ran to the top story and either shot people in the
street on the head or shot sparrows or broke neighbors' beautiful
panes of plate glass, and when they clattered, I could laugh right

heartily; well, I kept this up day after day, indeed I had learned to shoot the pea-shooter so accurately that I could kill a sparrow even at three hundred paces. I scared the carrion flock so much that upon hearing my name mentioned they knew what the score was. When now my Mother perceived that studying wouldn't sit with me and that she was paying tuition in vain she took me out of school and left me with a genteel merchant with whom I was supposed to become a famous business man; indeed I probably could have turned out so if only I had desired, for instead of taking notice of the numbers on the goods and of how dearly the yard would have to be sold for a profit, I always had other pranks in mind; and whenever my boss sent me somewhere for a speedy return, I never forgot to take my pea-shooter along, went up one street, down another, and looked for sparrows or for beautiful, large panes in windows where no one was watching; then I would smash them with a shot and then run along, and when I returned to my master after several hours' absence I would always tell him such nice prevarications that he never said anything to me his whole life. However I finally perceived that it wouldn't take much for him to smash my pea-shooter in two over my back, so I took warning, and pulled out with my pea-shooter, saying I would return. Then he sent word to my Mother that I caused him all sorts of trouble with people on account of my pea-shooter and wouldn't fit into business at all. My Mother sent word to the merchant that it was all right, she wouldn't leave me with him again, since I had run away from him and was with her again, perhaps I would show some interest in something better. Well, when my Mother answered the merchant thusly, that was water for my mill again and if before I hadn't bedeviled the people in the streets and beautiful window panes I really went after them now that I had my own way. When my Mother finally saw that complaints kept pouring in and that many people had to have windows replaced, she said to me: "Dear son Schelmuffsky, you're gradually getting better sense and growing nicely, do tell me what I should do with you since you show no interest whatever in anything and day after day do nothing but make enemies of my neighbors with your pea-shooter and cause me great trouble?" Whereupon I answered my Mother, saying: "Dear Mother, know something?

I want to get going to see foreign lands and cities, perhaps I shall become a famous fellow through my travels so that later, upon my return, everyone will have to put his hat under his arm before me if he wants to speak to me." My Mother liked this proposal and said that if I could accomplish this, I should indeed see something of the world; she would give me some money for the trip to sustain me for a while. Whereupon I was quick to get together what I wanted to take along, wrapped everything in a drill handkerchief, stuck it in my pants pocket, and made ready for the trip; yet I should like to have taken my pea-shooter too; however I didn't know how to do this, and feared that it might be stolen or taken en route, so I left same at home and hid it in the top story behind the chimney and set out on my very dangerous trip in my twenty-fourth year. What I now saw, heard, experienced, and withstood abroad by sea and land will be heard in the following chapter with the greatest astonishment.

# The Second Chapter

That same day the cuckoo began to call for the first time in the year as I took leave of my Mother in Schelmerode, fell on her neck, embraced her thrice on each cheek, then wandered out through the city gate. Zounds! Outside the gate how vast the world seemed, I didn't know, the devil take me, whether to march westward or in the direction of the sunset; indeed, ten times I was of a will to turn around and remain with my Mother, if only I hadn't taken such a burdensome oath not to return to her before I had become a fine fellow, and yet I shouldn't have paid too much attention to the oath either, since I previously had taken oaths and not kept them, but surely should have wandered back to my Mother's house if a count had not come driving up to me across the field on a sleigh and asked me why I was standing there so pensive; whereupon I answered the count, that I wanted to see the world, but that everything seemed so vast, I didn't know how I should begin. Answering me, the count replied: "*Monsieur*, there is something striking about your eyes, and as you want to see the world, sit down beside me in my bell sleigh and ride with me, for I too am traveling about the world to see what's going on here and there." As soon as the count had said this, I jumped at once with both legs into his bell sleigh and, to prevent freezing, stuck my right hand into my trousers in front and my left into my right coat pocket, for the wind was blowing very cold and had frozen ice yardthick that same night; yet it was good that we had the wind behind us, because it couldn't get at me so, because the count, who was sitting in back on the back seat and driving, retarded it a little, thus we drove out southward to see the world. En route we told about ourselves; beginning, the count told of his countly condition, that he stemmed from an ancient family with thirty-two forefathers; and he likewise told me the village where his grandmother was buried, but I forget it again, then he chattered to me also how he as a young boy of sixteen always thoroughly enjoyed catching birds and how he once had thirty-one titmice roasted in butter which he had caught in a snare and how he had enjoyed eating them. After he had related the course of his life from beginning to end I began to chatter about my astonishing birth and how the rat had acted after it had devoured my Mother's quite new silk dress and had

run between my sister's legs and unexpectedly got into the hole
where it should have been beaten to death; also about my pea-
shooter with which I could shoot so accurately, zounds! How the
count opened up his mouth and nose at this when I told him such
things and opined that I would make something of myself in the
world. After such relation we came to a tavern which was situated in the open field hard by the road, here we got out and went
in to warm ourselves up a little; as soon as we came in the count
ordered a large glass which in these parts held about eighteen
to twenty measures; he had the innkeeper fill it full and proposed that we should drop formalities of speech. Now I had not
supposed that the count would drink down the whole glass full
of brandy all at once, however, the devil take me, he did drink it
clean down in one slurp without pausing or wiping his beard so
that even the innkeeper was terribly astonished. Then he had
it filled likewise full again for me and said: "Well, *allons*, brother Schelmuffsky, you're a cur if you don't drink it down like
me." Zounds, this business irked me to have the count throw
such words around so fast, so I began to speak: "Right, brother,
I'll keep up with you." At this answer the innkeeper began to
smile scornfully toward the count and opined I couldn't possibly
keep up with him because the count was a fat, corpulent gentleman compared with whom I was only an upstart into whose
stomach the glass of brandy could hardly go. However I was
quick to seize the glass of brandy and drank it down rapidly, the
devil take me, in one gulp. Zounds! How the innkeeper opened
his pair of eyes and murmured furtively to the count that I must
amount to something. Whereupon the count clapped me on the
shoulders right away and said: "Brother, pardon my urging you
to drink, henceforth there shall be no more of this, I now realize
how you are to be treated and people of your *conduite* can
hardly be found in the world." Replying very nicely to my brother the count, I remarked that I was forsooth a fine fellow and
should indeed soon amount to something when I should see more
of the world, and if he would remain my brother and friend,
he should spare me such things in the future. Zounds! How the
count humbled himself, begging me on bended knees, and saying
that he would be guilty of no more such excesses. Whereupon we
paid the innkeeper, got into our bell sleigh again and kept on
driving out into the world. At the end of October, when it had
turned quite dark, we arrived in the famous city of Hamburg

where we put up with our sleigh in a large house on the Horse Market where many aristocratic persons of quality and ladies were lodging. No sooner had we got out there than two Italian noblemen came down the stairs from above, one held a brass candlestick in his hand in which a lit candle was burning and the other a large burning lamp of earthenware which was overflowing with olive oil; they welcomed us and were pleased with my good health as well as with that of my brother the count. After thus complimenting us, the nobleman with the burning candle took me by the hand while the other with the burning olive oil lamp took the count by the sleeve and led us up the stairs so that we shouldn't fall, for six steps were broken at the top. Having now ascended the stairs we found an excellent, beautiful banquet hall decorated with the most beautiful tapestries and precious stones shimmering and flaming with gold and silver; in this same hall now stood two aristocratic Dutch dignitaries and two Portuguese ambassadors, they stepped forward to me and my brother the count likewise, bade us welcome and were likewise pleased at our good health and fortunate arrival; answering them forthwith very nicely, I said that their well being and health were likewise very pleasing to me and the count. After I had now presented my counter-*compliment*, the innkeeper appeared too in a green velvet fur jacket with a large ring of keys in his hand, bade us welcome likewise and inquired whether the count and I would please to accompany him up another flight where he would show us our room. Whereupon I and my Brother took leave of the whole company with a very nice countenance and followed the innkeeper so that he might show us the room which we were to occupy for our convenience. Accompanying him now up another flight, he unlocked an excellent, beautiful room in which stood a bed *galant* beyond all measure and in which everything was very well decked out, there he bade us make use of our convenience and if we needed anything merely to whistle down through the window, at which the house boy would be at our service immediately, whereupon he took leave of us. As soon as the innkeeper had turned his back, I was quick to pull off my shoes and stockings forthwith, and whistled to the house boy that he must bring me a pail of fresh water so that I could wash my feet for they stank horribly. The black velvet trousers of my brother the count had pulled a seam in the crotch, so he whistled to the chamber maid that she must bring him a needle with a string of white thread so that he could mend same again. There we now both sat, I washed my stinking feet, and my brother the count patched his ripped velvet trousers which looked very nice. After we had thus improved ourselves a bit, the innkeeper in his green velvet fur jacket came up to us again to summon us to the evening meal, whereupon I and my brother the count forthwith accompanied him; he led us down the stairs again across the beautiful hall into a large room where a long table stood decked, upon which the most splendid foods were set. The innkeeper requested us to tarry a little, the other gentlemen as well as ladies would soon be present to keep us company. It hardly took as long for him to say this before the two Italian noblemen who had previously complimented us trod into the dining room, likewise the two Dutch dignitaries and the two Portuguese ambassadors and each led in an aristocratic *dame* by the hand. Zounds! Seeing me and my brother the count standing there, how they made reverences to us, and especially the females, they looked at us, the devil take me, rightly amazed. The whole company which was to dine now being assembled, they urged me and my brother the count to occupy the place of honor at the head of the table, which we proceeded to do without hesitation; so I sat in the first place of honor, by me to my left sat my brother the count, and by me on my right at the corner sat the aristocratic *dames*, farther down, the others had all taken their proper places. During the meal now all kinds of affairs of state were discussed; I and my brother the count however kept stone silent and observed what was passing onto our plates, for in three days we had seen no bit of bread; but having both stuffed ourselves substantially fat, I then began to relate my astonishing birth and what had happened to the rat after it should have been beaten to death on account of the silk dress it had devoured. Zounds! How they all opened up their mouths and noses as I told such things, and looked at me with the greatest amazement. The aristocratic *dames* immediately began to toast my health which example the whole company followed; soon one lady, drinking, said: "Long live the aristocratic Lord of Schelmuffsky," another *dame* soon added: "Long live the aristocratic woman of quality who guarantees his birth by the name Schelmuffsky." All the time I turned a very nice countenance toward the females as they thus toasted me in turn. One aristocratic *dame* who quickly sat down by me on my right at the corner of the table had completely fallen in love with me on account of the incident of the rat. She meant so well with me that she pressed her fists across the table against me over a hundred times and also kept nudging her knee against mine because she was so very much in love with me, yet this was not difficult to understand because I was sitting so nicely next to her and everybody was, the devil take me, laughing with me at once. After I had now finished with my relation, my Brother forthwith began to chatter of his origin and whence his thirty-two forefathers all came, and also told in which village his Grandmother was buried, and how he as a young boy of sixteen had caught thirty-one titmice all at once in a snare and whatever else there was to it; but he mixed everything up so strangely, and confused a hundred with a thousand, and couldn't talk very well either on account of stammering so much that he soon stopped still in the middle of his tale when he saw that no one was even listening to him and observed what good things lay on his plate· But whenever I began to discourse, zounds! How they all listened like little mice, for my language was so charming and I could present everything with such a nice countenance that they listened, the devil take me, with nothing but pleasure.

The innkeeper now perceiving that nobody was eating and that the plates were pretty well polished, he had the table cleared again; this done, I and my brother the count complimented very nicely the entire company and rose from the table; when they now perceived this around the table, they all began to rise also. I and my brother the count then without hesitation made our way first out of the dining room and marched to our room. But the whole company accompanied us across the beautiful hall to our stairs where we had to go up, and there the company bade us good night and wished us a pleasant repose. I then returned them a nice *compliment*, saying that I was a fine fellow who was somewhat tired as well as the count, and that for several weeks we had had no bed, hence we doubted not at all that we should sleep stoutly and we hoped that they too should sleep well. Now after this very nicely presented answer, each went his way, I and my brother the count forthwith betook ourselves to the top of the flight to our room, and when we came in there, I whistled to the house boy that he should bring us a candle; he immediately appeared therewith and again went his way. Then I and my brother the count undressed stark naked and perceived what a fine thing had taken place in our shirts:

Zounds! How the sweat had come to life therein, we spent, the devil take me, over three whole clock hours before we could finish with the killing. Yet it wasn't so bad with me as with the count, he was, the devil take me, over twenty thousand stronger in numbers than I, so that after I had renovated my shirt, I had to help him for more than an hour before all the pests were snapped to death. Such necessary chore being accomplished, we lay down in the beautiful bed which stood in the room, but as soon as my brother the count rolled in, he forthwith began to snore so that I couldn't close one eye for the other on account of him, although right away I too was very tired and sleepy. As I now lay and listened for a little while, someone knocked quite softly on our door; I asked who was there, but no one would answer; again there was knocking, I asked again who was there, but no one would answer me. I was quick to leap out of bed naked, opened the door to see who was knocking; as I opened same, a female stood outside with a note in her hand, wished me in the darkness good evening, and inquired whether the aristocratic foreign gentleman who had told the incident of the rat at the table this evening had his room here. Hearing now that it was I myself, she went on: "Here is a note to you and I am to wait for a few lines in reply." I then had her give me the note, bade her wait a little by the door, quickly put on my shirt and trousers, and whistled to the house boy that he must light the candle for me, which he soon did. coming up the stairs with a large lantern, so I then broke open the note and saw what it contained. The contents were as follows:

### Charming Youth.

If it please you to look at my chamber yet this evening, let me know your answer by this *servante, adieu.*

Your affectionate lady
who sat by you this evening at the corner
of the table to your right and who
sometimes nudged your knee.

*La Charmante.*

Having now read this letter, I again whistled to the house boy that he must bring me a quill, ink, and paper; thereupon I sat down and wrote a very nice letter by way of answer to Lady *Charmante;* now it was composed like this:

> Anticipating everything dear and
> good, very honorable *Dame Charmante.*

Only first I want to put on my shoes and stockings as well as my coat again (for I already put on my shirt and trousers again, although I leaped out of bed naked when the *servante* was knocking as she brought me your letter, so I doubt that she saw much of me in the darkness) then I will come to you forthwith. However, very honorable *dame,* you must without fail send the *servante* back to me, that she may show me how I may find your chamber, and have her bring along a lantern, so that I may not fall in the dark either; for the devil take me, I'm not going to come alone. Why, it is now already between eleven and twelve, when the hangman commonly plays and a dread could easily befall me, so that by morning my mouth might be solidly distorted and how would you thereby be served if I got a whimpering mouth, therefore you know what care to take; if now, if you please, the female fetches me, well and good, if not, how quickly will I take off my trousers and shirt again, and lay me down in bed again by my brother the count. For the rest, farewell, I remain in return

> my very honorable *Madame Charmante's*
> ever most truly obedient, most obliging,
> most travel-ready
> Schelmuffsky.

I now sent this letter to the aristocratic *Dame Charmante* by way of answer, and quickly looked for my shoes and stockings under the bench, that I might put them on; I had hardly pulled one stocking onto my left leg when the *servante* again stood outside holding a large paper lantern in which an earthen lamp with two wicks was burning and wanted to light my way to *Dame Charmante's* chamber, so that I should not fall; now as soon as I had dressed, I put my sword, which was an excellent back scratcher, under my arm, and went along to *Charmante's* chamber. The *servante* was able to light my way quite well with the paper lantern; she led me from my room down the stairs again, across the beautiful hall, past a long passageway in the courtyard where I had to ascend six steps with her again before I

came to the chamber of *Charmante*. The female now showing
me the door, I forthwith unlatched it and stepped in unannounced without hesitation. When *Charmante* now saw me coming, she
forthwith leaped out of bed in her night *habit*, received me *à la
française* with a double kiss, and requested my pardon, to the
end that I might not be disinclined to accept such doings as her
sending for me late at night and troubling me to her chamber.
Answering *Charmante* hereupon very nicely, I said that I was
indeed a fine fellow the like of which one could hardly meet in
the world, and that it didn't matter since I couldn't fall asleep
anyway with my brother the count's snoring. When I answered
her thusly with a completely nice countenance, she bade me sit
by her on her bed and relate again the incident of the rat and
what kind of a hole it had really run into when one should have
beaten it to death with a broom on account of the devoured silk
dress.

Forthwith I told *Charmante* the whole incident, and said
concerning the hole into which the rat had run, that as a matter
of fact I had not seen the hole, but had been informed this much
by my sister, that when the rat had unexpectedly crept through
her legs it had disappeared, and thereupon no hangman could
have known where the gallows bird must have hidden forever and
eternally. Zounds! How the *Charmante* female fell on my neck
when she heard of this concealment, she stuck her tongue, the
devil take me, a whole half yard long into my mouth, so much
did she love me, and impressed one kiss after the other, cross-
wise on my mouth, so that I thought at times that heaven and
earth were weighing upon me, such was the extent of the pleasure of love which the female displayed for me. When now by
her all too great caresses she had indicated amorous inclinations
to me quite shamelessly, and I myself, the devil take me, didn't
know what I was doing, she then suggested wooing, and said I
should take her to wife; whereupon I replied however to *Charmante* very nicely, saying that as a matter of fact, I was a fine
fellow who would certainly amount to something after he had
seen more of the world, and that I was not so soon of a will to
take a wife. Yet I should not reject her, but should consider it a
little. Zounds! How the female began to howl and cry that I
should talk of giving her the gate, tears kept running down her
cheeks as if one were pouring tubs over her, and she made her
pair of eyes big as the biggest sheep.

If now for good or bad I didn't want her to howl herself to death over me, I had to, the devil take me, agree that I should want no one else but her for a wife; after this had now taken place, she was content again, whereupon she stuck her little tongue a whole half yard long into my mouth again and sucked with it in my throat as a small child on its mother's teat. After various such pleasures of love, I took leave of her the same evening, and had the *servante* with the paper lantern again light me to my room, and lay me down in bed by my brother the count, who was still lying there snoring away. I was hardly in bed again when I too got some of his mood, and there both of us were snoring like an old nag which had escaped from the knacker. Early the next day, possibly around nine o'clock, when I was in my best sleep, someone kicked scandalously at our door, so that I started up for terror fathom-high from my slumber. But the pounding would not cease; I was quick to leap out of bed forthwith with both legs, pulled on my shirt, and wanted to see who was there. As I opened up, the boy of the one Dutch dignitary stood there, asking whether this was the Lord of Schelmuffsky's room? When I answered the boy that it was I myself, he continued that his master would regard me as no fine fellow, but rather as an arch lazy-lout if I didn't appear on the big mead by the Altona Gate this forenoon by ten o'clock at the latest with a good sword, and there he would show me what *raison* was. Zounds! How it irked me to have the fellow say this to me through his boy. However I soon dismissed the boy with the following answer, saying: "Listen, you cur, go back to your master and tell him that I ask why he hadn't come to me himself and told me this, I should have soon polished him off; however in order that he see that I am not afraid of him, I will come and not only do him the favor of bringing a good sword, my back scratcher, but a pair of good pistols shall likewise be at his service, therewith I should show him how better to respect *Fortuna's* finest fellow the next time he might have something to pick a quarrel about." Thereupon the dignitary's boy went away, and didn't mutter another word except, coming to the stairs, he leered at me stealthily with a scornful countenance right sourly, and quickly ran down the stairs. But I was quick to go into the room again, dressed rapidly, and whistled to the house boy that he must come to me with the greatest speed. He then immediately presented himself to me instantaneously saying: "What is your Grace's pleasure?" I was right pleased that the fellow could answer me so discreetly. Whereupon I asked him whether he couldn't secure a pair of good pistols for me, such and such a thing was about to take place, he shouldn't come off the worse for this, and should understand that he might expect a tip for this. Zounds! When the fellow heard about the tip, how he sprang out the door, and in an instant appeared with a pair of wondrously beautiful pistols which were the innkeeper's; he had to load one for me with big buck shot, the other with small shot, and cap them with two balls; this being done, I girded my back scratcher to my side, the pistols I slipped into my belt, then marched ever silent towards the Altona Gate. Arrived at the gate, I now inquired forthwith where the big mead was. A little ship's boy soon informed me; when I had now walked a little piece from the city wall, I could see the big mead, and perceived that a big crowd of people stood there, towards whom I marched posthaste, and when I soon came to them, I saw that one dignitary was there with several others by him. But I asked him forthwith as I approached him whether he had challenged me here an hour ago through his boy and what the cause was; whereupon he answered me, yes, he had done this, and the cause was, because the previous night I had been with *Madame Charmante,* and he couldn't stand for this at all, that a stranger should serve her, whereupon he immediately had his sword blade out and was marching at me; when I now saw that he was older than I, zounds, how I unsheathed my back scratcher too, faced him, and had hardly parried his thrust before I delivered a pig thrust with my back scratcher and, the devil take me, using the fifth position, I scored on his left elbow so that the blood shot forth as thick as your arm, then I got at his body and, with the pistol which was heavily charged with small shot and balls, I was about to snuff out his life completely, and it would have happened at the height of my anger, if his comrades had not fallen upon my arms and begged me only to spare his life since I had had revenge enough. After considerable pleading, the matter was then settled so that I had to come to terms with him, with the stipulation that he should never trouble me any further by having his boy say such words to me if I should pay *Madame Charmante* a visit; he promised me this too; I can not describe enough, the devil take me, in what honor his comrades later held me, wherever an *action* was to take place, I always had to be present to regulate the disputants. For whenever I was not present at duels which were taking place covertly, no consideration was given to them, but when it was known that the Lord of Schelmuffsky seconded this one or that, then they all knew well enough how important the duel had been. Right away I related to *Dame Charmante* the *action* accomplished with the Dutch dignitary, and said that it had happened on her account; at first the female was very terrified at this, but when she heard how chivalrously I had conducted myself, she leaped up high for joy, fell on my neck, embraced me, and stuck her tongue deep into my mouth again which, the devil take me, pleased me right well on the part of the female. Thereupon I went up to the room to my brother the count who still lay in bed and listened; I told him also what had befallen me in Hamburg; now he was so angry that I hadn't wakened him; he would have liked to drive out in his bell sleigh and help me as my second, but I replied that a fine fellow must not be afraid of even hundreds of them. Thereupon the innkeeper in his green velvet fur jacket came up to us, and again summoned us to the noon meal. Zounds! How my brother the count leaped naked out of bed and dressed head over heels for fear of missing the meal; now after he had dressed, we both marched down to the table again with the innkeeper. The whole company which had dined with us the evening before appeared at the table again, excepting the one dignitary into whose arm I had thrust with the fifth position; he was not there, I and my brother the count without hesitation now again assumed the first place; I now thought that the *action* would be discussed somewhat at the table, however, the devil take me, not one word of this was mentioned, and I should not have recommended it to anyone either, for the fifth position and the pig thrust were still in my mind. They began to discourse again of all sorts of things, and thought that I would tell something again about which they could be amazed; they encouraged me too, but, the devil take me, I acted as if I didn't even notice it.

*Dame Charmante* began to drink my health, and the whole company followed suit. Then my brother the count began to tell of the titmice which he had caught all at once in the snare, and of how good they had tasted to him when his deceased grandmother had roasted them in butter for him. At which naive tale the whole company had to laugh. The meal finished, I sat in a carriage with my dearest *Charmante,* and we took a drive on the city wall of Hamburg to see how it was built, and indeed at some places it did not appear firm enough; I told the city *capitaine* vividly how it could be repaired in a quite different fashion. To be sure he wrote it down, but whether they have now done this, I am unable to say, for from that time on I didn't come there again. Hereafter we drove to the star redoubt and looked at this too. Zounds! How many bombs lay there which had been hurled in by the previous siege; I will wager that one probably weighed over three hundred hundredweight, I tried to see if I could lift up one with one hand, but, the devil take me, it wouldn't work, it was so heavy that I could hardly lift it up three yards with both hands. From here we drove out to the Elbe, and watched the ship boys fish there. Zounds, what trout they were catching there on their fish hooks; now they weren't for example such little trout as are found around in this country near Gutenbach or similar places, but, the devil take me, they were creatures of which one trout weighed a good twenty to thirty pounds; of these same fish I had eaten myself quite sate in Hamburg, and if at the present hour I still hear trout mentioned, I immediately feel quite sick from this. Why? In Hamburg they have no other fish than trout, year in year out, you have to get used to them whether you like or not; sometimes, at about the time of Candlemas, a few tuns of fresh herring arrive there, but still rather seldom, and besides what does that amount to? among such a crowd of people, the thousandth doesn't even get to see one of them. After I had watched the fishing a while with my dearest, we drove back to the city to our quarters; forthwith as we descended, a little hunched dancing master stood in the portal to the courtyard, and made a very nice *compliment* to *Madame Charmante* as well as to me, and invited us to a ball; my dearest *Charmante* asked me whether I desired to go there, for she couldn't turn the company down, and they probably would all be waiting for her. Answering, I said: "I'll come along all right and see what is going on there." Hereupon she informed the dancing master that she would be there right away. Zounds! How the fellow jumped about for joy, hearing that she would come and bring someone with her. He ran out of the house in the direction of the dance hall as if his head were burning. We immediately seated ourselves in our carriage and drove to the dance hall. As soon as we came up, zounds! What big goings on with the aristocratic ladies and cavaliers, who likewise had betaken themselves thither; there was a furtive whispering in the ears, and

I heard one begin with this: "Who can the aristocratic gentleman be whom *Madame Charmante* has brought along?" Then one lady said to another: "Isn't that a wonderfully handsome fellow, why he looks just like milk and blood." These and similar remarks went furtively around the company at the dance hall for a good half hour. The dancing master presented a red velvet chair to me, upon which I had to sit down, but the others as well as my *Charmante* all had to stand. Thereupon the music now began, zounds! How the fellows could play, they began with a popular song to which the little hunched dancing master danced the first *entrée*. Zounds! How the little fellow could leap, it seemed to me exactly as if he were flying in air, the devil take me. When this dance was over, they all formed a circle with one another, and began to dance serpentine; my *Charmante* was obliged to step into the circle now, and dance solo therein. Zounds! How the female could dance around serpentine so that, the devil take me, I thought every second now she's going to fall down; however it seemed as though nothing bothered her. The other girls danced *galamment* too, the devil take me, I can't say how nicely they could place their feet, but no one could equal my *Charmante*. After the serpentine circle dance was now over they began to dance all sorts of customary dances too like *courantes, chiques, allemandes,* and the like. I was now supposed to dance this stuff too; various *dames* came to the velvet chair upon which I sat, and invited me to a little dance too; at first to be sure I excused myself by saying what a fine fellow I was, from whose eyes to be sure something important was sparkling, but I had not yet really learned to dance. However, the devil take me, no excusing availed, the *dames* carried me along with the chair into the dance circle, and upset me from the chair, so that I fell supine, the devil take me, but I stood up with a very nice countenance again, so that the whole company was amazed at me, and one cavalier kept saying to the other that I surely must be one of the finest fellows in the world. Whereupon I now began to dance, taking three ladies, one had to grasp my left hand, the other the right, and the third had to hold on to my left foot, therewith I ordered the musicians to strike up the Altenburg peasants' dance. Then one really should see beautiful dancing, as I did such nice leaps on my right foot; when I now had thus warmed up a little, I leaped up on my leg fathoms high, the devil take me, so that the one lady who had clutched my left foot hardly touched the floor with

either foot, but continually hopped around in the air with me.
Zounds! How the females all looked as I did such leaps; the little
hunched dancing master vowed high and dear he had never seen
such leaps in all his life. Then they all wanted to know about my
family and origin, however, the devil take me, I told no one, to be
sure I identified myself only as an aristocrat of nobility, but they
wouldn't believe this, but I must be something much more aristocratic, for my eyes had already revealed that I sprang from no
hazel bush; they asked my *Charmante* also, but the hangman
would surely have taken her before she had mentioned anything
of my birth, for if they had heard the historie of the rat, zounds!
How they would have listened. The ball concluded, I rode with
my *Charmante* to the opera which, the devil take me, was beautiful to behold too, for that very day they were playing the destruc-
tion of Jerusalem. Zounds! What a great city that Jerusalem
was that they were presenting in the opera there; I will wager,
the devil take me, it was a good ten times bigger than the city
of Hamburg, and they destroyed the thing there so viciously too
that, the devil take me, you couldn't even see where it had stood.
Only it was ever and eternally too bad that the wondrously
beautiful temple of Solomon had to go to the dogs; methinks if
only a speck had been spared, but no, everything had to be
ruined and destroyed by those soldiers. It was Croats and
Swedes who thus ruined Jerusalem. This opera concluded, I
drove with my *Charmante* to the Jungfernstieg (as the Ham-
burgers call it), for it is a very merry place situated in the
center of the city of Hamburg on a little water called the Elster;
there stand a good two thousand lindens, and every evening the
most aristocratic cavaliers and ladies of the city of Hamburg
promenade there and take fresh air under the lindens; now I
was to be found there at this same Jungfernstieg each evening
with my dearest *Charmante*. For the Jungfernstieg and the opera house were always our best means of passing the time. They
also once played an opera about the siege of Vienna which was
excellent to see. Zounds, what bombs the Turks hurled into the
city of Vienna, they were, the devil take me, twenty times bigger
than those which lie in the star redoubt mentioned at Hamburg.
However they will probably know best how they were paid for
this by the Saxons and Polacks. For I suppose over thirty thousand men of the Turks remained on the spot, not counting those
taken prisoner and mortally wounded, so I estimate approxi-

mately eighteen to twenty-two thousand men, and a good forty thousand took to flight. Zounds! How the trumpets sounded, how shocked was the city; I'll wager probably over twenty thousand trumpeteers worked together to sound *Victoria*. With such diversion then did I and my *Charmante* daily while away our time in Hamburg, but what it cost me in money I won't say to anyone, the devil take me, but I rue no farthing squandered with *Charmante*, for she was an excellently beautiful female, and to please her I would have doffed and pawned my trousers should there have been a dearth of money, for she loved me completely, and called me only her charming youth, for at that time I was far more handsome than now. Why? You will hear later how the sun below the equator burned me so viciously. Yes, Hamburg, when I think of it still, Hamburg gave me much pleasure. And, the devil take me, I should not have left it so soon either (although I had been taking a look at it now for three full years) if my back scratcher hadn't made me so unlucky. Which to be sure was because of my dearest *Charmante,* yet the good female couldn't help it either that I had to sneak out by night and fog. For a fine fellow dare not let himself be defied. The whole affair however was like this: I was invited with my *Charmante* to a merry party, and was obliged to remain there in the evening at the same aristocratic place where the company was; having now eaten, it was already very late at night, we were therefore requested to stay, but my *Charmante* wouldn't sleep there; however the aristocratic man where we were had his carriage hitched to take us to our quarters, that we might suffer no harm; but soon arrived at the Horse Market, my *Charmante* asked me to ride with her for another half hour through the Jungfernstieg, she only wanted to see what kind of company would be found there. I obliged her, and ordered the coachman to drive us thither. But not far from the Jungfernstieg, as we were obliged to drive through a narrow little street, some persons began to hurl challenges in the aforesaid street. Now my blood began to boil whenever someone approached me with a chip on his shoulder, and I should have liked it ten times better, the devil take me, if someone had delivered a rude thrust at me, rather than charging up to me with such challenges. I was quick to tell my *Charmante* she should have the coachman turn about and drive to her quarters, I would see for whom this affront was intended, and it was impossibly acceptable that they should thus challenge

and insult the finest fellow of *Fortuna*. But my *Charmante* didn't
want to let me go; fearing I might have misfortune, she fell upon
my neck, embraced me, and again stuck her tongue way deep
into my mouth, so earnestly did she desire me to stay with her;
however before she realized it, I jumped out of the carriage with
both legs, ordered the coachman to turn about, and then marched
after the nocturnal challengers, whom I met still at the end of
the narrow little street and began with them, who were a good
thirty in number: "What are you lazy louts challenging about?"
But the fellows closed in on me with bared swords, thinking I
should be afraid of them. To be sure I retreated a step, then when
I had whipped out my back scratcher, zounds! How I hewed and
thrust at the fellows, it was just as if I were chopping cabbage
and turnips: fifteen of them remained right on the spot, some of
these whom I had wounded seriously asked for quarter, and others dashed away crying for the watch. Zounds, when I heard the
word watch, I thought, this business might not turn out well for
you if they should seize you; I was quick to keep marching rapidly
to the Altona Gate, where I gave the gate watchman a whole double thaler to oblige him to let me pass through the wicket gate.
Outside I now sat me down on the very mead where I with the
fifth position had thrust through the left elbow of the one Dutch
dignitary and cried there like a little snotnose. Being now cried
out, I stood up, faced toward the city of Hamburg again to see
whether I could view it again even in the dark and said: "Well,
good night, Hamburg, good night, Jungfernstieg, good night,
opera house, good night, brother count, and good night, my dearest *Charmante*, only don't pine to death because your charming
youth must leave you, mayhap you will get to see him again soon
elsewhere." Hereupon I walked away in the dark and ever into
the world. By early morning I arrived in the city of Altona, which
is situated three long German miles from Hamburg, there I put
up at the most aristocratic inn called At the Sign of the Vineyard, in which I met a countryman who was sitting in the warm
spot behind the tile stove with two aristocratic *dames* by him,
whom he was cheating at cards and everything. I told him about
myself and how I had fared in Hamburg. He was, the devil take
me, a fine fellow also, for he had come from France only several
days ago, and was awaiting here a bill of exchange at the innkeeper's in the Vineyard, which his Mother should send him
at the earliest opportunity. He showed me very great honor that

I shall extol my lifelong, the devil take me, and also counseled me not to tarry long in Altona; if it should become known in Hamburg that so and so who had made so many souls kaputt was staying here, the watch would surely be sent after me to seize my head, even though it be in another district. Which good counsel I followed too, and because that very day a ship was sailing from there for the land of Sweden, I took passage on same, took leave of my countryman, and marched away from Altona. What now happened to me then at sea, what I saw and experienced in the land of Sweden, will be heard quite nicely in the following chapter.

# The Third Chapter

It was just in the midst of Whitsuntide that I first betook me to sea; now I had thought the ships at Hamburg big which people were wont to sail on at the Jungfernstieg, but I soon perceived that the ones at sea by Altona, the devil take me, were still a thousand times bigger, for people called them great freighters; having taken leave of my countryman, I now embarked on one such and sailed away. Hardly had I sailed a half hour to sea before I became ill with sea sickness. Zounds! How I began to vomit, I felt exactly as though, the devil take me, my innards would all have to come out of my body, for there was no end at all, and it kept up three whole days and nights on the ship; the others were all amazed at my having to produce so much stuff; early the fourth day, as I now gradually began to feel a little better, I had the skipper give me a glass of brandy of about twelve measures. I now quickly tossed down same in one gulp, thinking it would cure my stomach again. Zounds! When I got that stuff into my body, how sick I began to get again, and if I had not vomited before, I really threw up after the brandy, with the result that after again regurgitating without surcease four whole days, the devil take me, the following fifth day, the clear goat's milk came up which I had drunk from childhood up to my twelfth year, and which must have caught somewhere in my body for so long; after such was now out of my body, and I had nothing more at all to throw up, the skipper bade me slurp down a good glass full of olive oil, that my stomach hereupon might again settle nicely and accommodatingly, which I proceeded to do, and slurped, the devil take me, well over fifteen tankards of olive oil into me with one gulp.

As soon as I had the stuff in my body, I felt better from that hour on. The thirteenth day around ten o'clock forenoon, it became black as pitch, so that you couldn't even see a stitch, and the captain had to hang out a big lantern on the front of the ship, that he might know whither he was sailing, for he surely didn't dare to trust his compass, it faltered repeatedly. Towards evening then, zounds, such a storm arose at sea that we just thought we should all have to perish. The devil take me, I suppose I can say that it seemed to us exactly in such a storm as if we were being rocked in a cradle as little children; the captain probably

would have liked to anchor, but there was no bottom, so he had
to take care that he didn't sail his ship onto a reef. The nineteenth day the sky began to clear again gradually, and the storm
settled so quickly, that the twentieth day became quiet, with
good weather, better than we ourselves wished. Also after this
storm the water in the sea became so clear that, the devil take
me, you could see all the fish swimming in the sea. Zounds! What
sticklebacks! One stickleback there was, the devil take me, as big
as the biggest salmon here on land, and pike? The devil take me,
they had tongues hanging out of their snouts like big Polish oxen;
among others you could also see fish there with horrible, big,
red eyes; I will wager that an eye on such a fish was almost bigger than the bottom of a vat here on land in which people are
wont to brew good sticky beer. I asked the skipper what they
called the fish, he said they just called them big-eyes. At the end
of the same month we smelled land, and the following month we
got to see the spires of the beautiful towers in Stockholm toward
which we were sailing; when now we were still about a mile from
the city, we sailed quite smoothly along the shore. Zounds! How
beautiful are the meads about Stockholm; people were just hay-
ing at this very time, they walked in the grass, the devil take me,
up to their arms, it was pure joy to see it; there were probably
over six thousand hay doodles that they had already stacked on
one mead there. Having now arrived quite near to the city the
captain stopped, bade us pay our fare and debark, which we did.
Now debarked there on shore, one went this way, another that;
I now wandered right into the city and, not wishing to lodge in
any common inn, I stayed in the suburb and took my quarters
with a fancy gardener who was, the devil take me, quite a solid
fellow. Now as soon as I reported to him, requesting quarters, he
said yes forthwith; whereupon I immediately told him of my
birth and the incident of the rat. Zounds! What a pleasure for
the man to hear these things, the devil take me, he was so polite
towards me and always kept his little cap under his arm in addressing me, for he called me nothing but Your Grace. Now he
also surely perceived that I was a fine fellow, and that there
must be something important about me. He had an excellent,
beautiful garden; now almost daily the most aristocratic persons
from the city drove out to his place for a promenade. Although
I suppose I wished to stay there incognito without revealing myself and my position, nevertheless I was soon discovered. Zounds!

What *visites* didn't I have from the most aristocratic *dames* in Stockholm; the devil take me, every day I suppose thirty carriages full kept driving into the garden merely in order to see me, for the fancy gardener had probably extolled to the people what a fine fellow I was. Among others, one lady kept driving to the garden, her father was the most aristocratic man of the city, people just called her Mistress Lisette; the devil take me, she was an excellently beautiful female, now she had fallen mortally in love with me, and really gave me to understand that I should woo and marry her. Whereupon answering her very nicely, I said that I was a fine fellow whose eyes showed something of importance, that therefore for the present she could be supplied with no certain answer. Zounds! How the female began to howl and cry as I gave her the gate; well, the devil take me, I didn't know what to do with her. Finally I began to answer her, saying that I was already half and half betrothed to a girl in Hamburg, however I had no post from her whether she was still alive or dead, she should only be patient, in several days I would give her an answer, whether or not I would marry her. Wherewith she was content again, and fell onto my neck and was so fond of me, the devil take me, that I had completely resolved to let *Charmante* go, and hold to Mistress Lisette. Whereupon taking leave of me with crying eyes, she said she would call upon me again early the next morning, and therewith drove into the city to her parents. What happened? The following morning came, I had a good fresh milk prepared, with which I would treat Mistress Lisette in the garden; the forenoon past, the afternoon was likewise almost over, I kept waiting in the garden with the fresh milk, but no Mistress Lisette would come, so that, the devil take me, because I was so crazed, and couldn't contain myself, I let the fresh milk get into my hair and ate it up solely for spite. As I now was putting the last spoonful into my mouth, the gardener's boy ran quickly into the garden, and asked me if I knew the news? As I was now eager to hear what there was, he began, that Mistress Lisette, who had been so long in the garden with me yesterday evening, had suddenly died tonight. Zounds! How I started at this post, the last spoonful of milk forthwith congealed in my throat. Yes (the boy continued) and they say the doctor said she must have been sorely grieved about something, otherwise she surely would not have died, since no illness at all was discernible in her. Zounds! How I pitied the female, and there was, the devil take me, surely no one responsible for her death but me for not wanting to marry her. I felt sorry for the female very long, the devil take me, before I could forget her; in her honor I had a poet compose the following lines, and had them cut on her tombstone, which even now may still be read on her grave in Stockholm:

> Wanderer hurried, stay and contemplate this stone
> and guess who here may lie buried all alone:
> For pain of love died Lis', petite on her couchette
> Now guess who lies herein: the lovely child Lisette.

After this little Lisa, the daughter of an aristocratic noble then fell in love with me; her name was Damigen, and she likewise now gave me to understand that she was interested in wooing. The devil take me, she too was an incomparable female. I was obliged to drive around with her every day and ever be with her; now although to be sure I was much given to the noble's daughter, and had likewise given a vain promise of marrying her, nevertheless I had not yet taken the formal step, yet all the little street boys ran around calling that Mistress Damigen was engaged, how well she was doing, that she was getting such an aristocratic fine fellow for a husband, at whom everybody forthwith laughed whenever they saw him. Now the whole city was full of such long-winded chatter. I had quite resolved to marry her, and would have taken her too, if her father had not promised her to another noble without the knowledge and consent of me or her. What happened? Damigen asked me to take her walking through the city of a Sunday that people just might see, for they had heard from the fancy gardener that I was such a fine, excellent fellow from whose eyes nothing common sparkled, so many of them sorely yearned merely to have a look at me. Now I could easily do her the favor of showing her about the city a little. St Baldwin's day just happened to fall on a Sunday when I went walking with Damigen about the city of Stockholm, leading her by the hand; when the people now saw that I was proudly walking along there with my Damigen, zounds, how they leaned over their window sills! They kept speaking furtively to one another, and as much as I could hear, first one said "Why, he's a wondrously handsome fellow!" Then someone from another house said: "I've never seen the like of him my livelong days!" Again, a pair of little boys stood there, saying to each other: "Hey, you, look, here comes the female who's getting the aristo-

cratic, rich junker who lodges out there at the fancy gardener's."
Then a pair of maids at a corner said: "Oh, people, just think
how well Mistress Damigen is doing, she's getting that fellow
there who is leading her by the hand, the female doesn't even de-
serve him." People were now furtively making these and similar
remarks to one another. Also, there was such a gawking after us,
the devil take me, I can't describe it. When we now came to the
market, and tarried there a bit, that I might rightly see the
people, that same noble may see this, that I am there conducting
Damigen around with complete pleasure whom he was supposed
to have as his beloved; however I didn't notice that the fellow
will undertake such a foolish thing. As people now were looking
at me and my Damigen in great astonishment, he came up from
behind, and delivered such a thrust at me, that, the devil take
me, my hat flew far from my head, then he quickly ran into a
house. Zounds! How I ground my teeth to think that the fellow
dared to do such a thing, and if he had not run off, I should have
thrust him through the heart with the fifth position, the devil
take me, so that he would surely forget to stand up. Also I was of
a will to follow him if Damigen had not kept me back; she said
it might cause such a big to-do with people and I could find him
all right at another time. Damigen having made this suggestion,
I donned my hat again in such a nice *manière* that everyone who
had seen the thrust delivered to me from behind furtively said
to one another there must be something important about me.
Even though I now deported myself toward Damigen as if it
were of no matter to me, still I could not cease grinding my teeth,
so crazed I was that I finally asked Damigen whether, if it pleased her, we shouldn't wander out to the fancy gardener's again
and divert ourselves there a bit in the garden. Damigen obeyed
me completely, we both walked back again in such a nice *manière*
toward the fancy gardener's house where I sat me down in the
grass with my Damigen and counseled her how I should go about
avenging myself with the noble. Thereafter Damigen entered
her coach and drove back into the city to her house. The following
day, having inquired where the fellow who had boxed my ears
dwelled, I sent the gardener's boy to him and had him say that I
considered him no fine fellow, but rather the most miserable of
all lazy louts in the world if he didn't present himself with a pair
of good pistols at such and such a time out there on the great
mead, and there I would show him I was a fine fellow. What

happens when the fancy gardener's boy now rubs these words under the nose of the noble and prattles of pistols, zounds! The fellow is so terrified, he doesn't know how to answer the boy. When now the boy inquires what answer he should bring back then to the aristocratic gentleman, he finally begins to speak, he must indeed admit that he knocked the hat off my head; it had so vexed him to see me leading his dearest to be, Mistress Damigen, by the hand, and he could not stand this at all. Although I was now forthwith challenging him with pistols on account of the ear-boxing, he would hardly come, because it was like this with shots, how easily he or I could receive something of them, and how would we then be afterward; and therefore he would not come, but if I would fight him with bare fists, then he would first ask his mother if she would allow this. However if she should not grant him this, he could give me no *revanche* for the ear-boxing. Zounds! When the boy brought me back such an answer from the noble, I should like to have thrust and cut at him immediately. I was quick to consider how I would treat him again. At first I was of a will to knock him down on the street and walk away, but then I thought, where will your Damigen then seek you; finally I resolved to repay him the thrust doubly in public company, and throw him down weightily with my Spanish stick. I would have done this too, if the fellow had not forthwith made such a great to-do on account of the challenge by pistol, that I was thus requested by high authority to let things be; enough that they all knew that I was a fine fellow, few of the like of whom would scarely be found in the world. Hearing this, that high authority requested me to let him be, and let myself be considered the finest fellow in the world, I should then probably not have troubled myself to think of him again. However I wasn't getting my Damigen either, to be sure her father let me know he well perceived that I was a fine fellow, the like of whom one scarcely found, but he had promised his daughter to a noble, and whoever was not noble dare not imagine that he would get her. Whereupon I let him be informed nicely, that as a matter of fact he had spoken quite rightly in calling me a fine fellow, few of the like of whom were to be met in the world, and indeed I had never yet demanded his daughter, but rather she would have me. When the old noble questions his Damigen about this, she says yes, it is true and yet she will not take him whom one would force upon her; if she should not have me, she would take none at all, and she would rather do something else than marry someone whom she couldn't love. But thereupon Damigen's father watched her sharply and forbade her upon his highest displeasure to drive out to me again, for he likewise had arranged at all gates that no one should let her out. If then I thus didn't get to see Damigen again, afterward the good female was quite unhappy, so that everyone thought ill of her stern lord and father for denying her to me. Thereafter I had quite resolved to leave Stockholm again since I already had looked around there two whole years. Resolved now to betake myself to ship again the next day, I took one more walk the previous day in the gardener's ornamental park to see if the plums were soon ripe. While I was examining one tree after another, the gardener's boy quickly ran up to me, saying that someone stopping outside by the gate with a beautiful bell sleigh would like to speak with me. He was wearing a large, green fox fur. Now I could not think fast who this must be, finally I recalled my brother the count, wondering whether it must not be he, and quickly ran with the boy out of the garden; as I came up it was, the devil take me, my brother the count whom I had left in the lurch in Hamburg. Zounds, how happy we both were to see each other. I took him forthwith into the gardener's room and right away had him given something to eat and drink, for, the devil take me, he was quite starved, and his horse looked quite meager also; the gardener's boy forthwith had to ride him out to the meadows in the pasture that he should have his fill again. Therewith he related to me all sorts of things, how he had fared in Hamburg, and how Lady *Charmante* had missed me so when I had had to take flight and leave her so unexpectedly. He also brought along a letter to me from her which she had only written me forlorn, that he nevertheless might deliver it to me, for she had thought I was long since dead, since I had not written her at all where I was. The contents of the letter were as follows and versewise:

### Charming Youth

are you still alive? Or do you lie buried?
Send you neither letter nor greeting to your dearest?
Ah the saying is, right in vain for that to have tarried,
Which one kisses in thought must long since be mouldy at best.

Are you then dead? So grant I you herewith the most joyous pleasures,

Do you still live, my charming sweet? And look now at this sheet

Which *Charmante* sends who had t'avoid you with sudden measures,

When your hero's bravery did you from the town speed.

Live you still? Then I do please implore, write me back importune,

Where you are, no matter may the way dangerous wend,

For you I will implore heaven's goodly, fast fortune,

If forthwith now to your *Charmante* first merely a word you send.

When I had read this letter, *Charmante* touched my heart so that I could not refrain from crying, but bade my brother the count eat, and went out the door and cried, the devil take me, like a little boy; being then cried out I asked the gardener to give me quill and ink, I would answer this letter as fast as possible. The fancy gardener replied that all this could be found above in the summer room, and if I desired, he would have it fetched down, but if it pleased me to write up there where I would not be disturbed by talking, I could do that too. That I accepted, requesting my brother the count to excuse me while I left him alone a little, and I was concerned only with answering and sending off the letter. Whereupon my brother the count said I should make no fuss about him, I might write as long as I would, he would not hinder me. Whereupon I wandered out the door and wanted to run up the stairs as fast as possible, but failing to notice a broken tread, I fall there with my right leg into the hole where the step is missing and, the devil take me, forthwith fragilely break my leg in two. Zounds! How I began to shriek! They all, including the count, came running up and asked what had happened to me, but no one could help me, the leg was simply in pieces. The fancy gardener immediately sent for the executioner to come and bind me, for he was, the devil take me, a solid man for healing fractures; he fixed me up again very nicely, even though he doctored thereon a good twelve weeks. When now I could step a little on it again, I had to answer *Charmante's* letter first of all which was composed very nicely also versewise as follows:

With the wish first of all for everything dear and good,
Schelmuffsky's living yet and in very good mood!
Though twelve weeks ago the right leg he has broken,
Yet the executioner's healing art will soon give a good
token.
My brother the count safe in his sleigh has come to me here
with Godspeed,
A letter he's brought me from which I now read,
*Charmante* my dear would like to know, live I yet or be
dead?
The devil take me, for there's yet neither need nor dread.
I'm living now in Swedish country,
Would you now like dear child with me to parley?
With the fancy gardener in Stockholm's suburb I do now
reside,
So soon must you come to my side,
For here intend I not still longer to repose.
This is the import of that which I did want as answer fine
for you to compose.
Meanwhile fare well, healthy, pert both late and early
And I shall remain forever your
                    charming youth
                        Schelmuffsky.

Now although I had never made any pretention to poetasting, nevertheless, the devil take me, this letter turned out for me
versewise very nicely. I now sent same by the gardener's boy to
the posthouse in Stockholm that it might be dispatched *cito* to
Hamburg. Then had hardly four weeks ensued before my dearest
*Charmante* showed up too. Seeing me now, zounds, the female
fell onto my neck and hugged me, indeed she almost gobbled up
my mouth, the devil take me. Then she also told me how the
Hamburg watch had searched for me in her bed three times because I chopped so many fellows to ruin, and how the company
at the dancing hall had missed me so because I was such an excellent leaper. I should tell her too how I had fared during the
time after my forced flight from Hamburg. That I told her, also
how we had had a storm at sea, and of the various fish I had
seen, but, the devil take me, I told nothing of how I had fared in
Stockholm in connection with the ear-boxing on account of Mistress Damigen. Although I now would fain set sail again to have

a further look at the world, since my foot again was completely
cured, nevertheless I let *Charmante* persuade me to remain
another half year in Stockholm to show her this and that. Now
there is nothing especial to see there, except that Stockholm is
a fine city very pleasantly situated, about which are cultivated
beautiful gardens, meads, and excellent vineyards and that,
the devil take me, the most beautiful wine is made there.
But of fisheries and such things there are as few as in Hamburg.
To be sure they have enough trout there too, but who can always
eat the same fish; however there is unprecedented cattle breed-
ing there because of the grazing; there are, the devil take me,
cows there of which one may give forty to fifty tankards of milk
at one time. In winter they make butter fast too, it looks like the
most beautiful spun wax, the devil take me. Having now
conducted my *Charmante* everywhere about and shown her
this and that in Stockholm, I again prepared for the trip with
her and my brother the count, payed for what I had consumed
at the fancy gardener's, and we took passage on a ship which
should take us to Holland. After we were set with the ship, the
count packed his bell sleigh with his horse aboard so that, coming to land, he could drive again. It being almost time for the
ship to sail away, we took leave of the fancy gardener, thanking
again for all favor shown. Whereupon, the devil take me, the
man began to cry like a little child, our departure grieved him
so. As a final gesture he presented me with a wondrously
beautiful flower; even though this flower had coal-black leaves,
you could nevertheless smell it, the devil take me, at a whole
mile's distance. He called it simply violet kohlrabi, and I now
took this violet kohlrabi along. Whereupon we now marched
away toward our ship; arrived there, zounds, what a crowd likewise bound for Holland was there, the devil take me, there were
well nigh six thousand souls who now came aboard likewise of
a will to see Holland. How we now fared miserably at sea will
make your hair stand on end when you read the following
chapter.

# The Fourth Chapter

When we sailed from Stockholm it was just at the time when the cherries and grapes were beginning to color. Zounds! What a crowding and squeezing with so many people aboard. I and my dearest *Charmante*, likewise my brother the count, had a room for our own convenience on the ship because the captain saw that we were persons of quality. But the other six thousand, the devil take me, were obliged to take turns sleeping on pallets of straw. For several weeks we sailed very happily and were all right merry aboard; but then we came to the isle of Bornholm, where there are so many reefs that if a captain doesn't know his way he can very easily capsize. Zounds! What a great storm and turbulence suddenly arose at sea, the wind beat the waves up as high as towers over the ship, and it began to grow dark as coal. As the greatest misfortune of all however he had left and forgotten the compass on an inn table in Stockholm, so that consequently he knew not at all where he was, and whither he should sail. The raging and roaring of the cruel turbulence lasted fourteen full days and nights, the fifteenth day, when we thought things would quiet down a bit, a storm arose again, and the wind drove our ship onto a reef so that it quickly broke, the devil take me, into one hundred thousand pieces. Zounds! What a situation there at sea! In an instant ship, captain, everyone who had been aboard, went down, and if I and my brother the count had not quickly seized a plank upon which we forthwith placed ourselves so that we could float, no other means could have helped us, and we should have had to perish likewise with the six thousand souls; zounds! what a lamentation the people set up in the water, nothing saddens me so up to the present hour as the thought of my dearest of all *Charmante;* whenever I think of that female my eyes still overflow, the devil take me. For I heard her still calling about ten times "charming youth" in the water, but how could I help her, the devil take me, I had all I could do to keep from falling off the plank, not to mention the fact that I should have helped her. It was ever and eternally a pity that that female unexpectedly had to risk her life; the devil take me, not a single soul could save itself except me and the count on the plank. After now viewing this tragedy from our plank at a distance for awhile, I and my brother the count paddled it away with our hands and were obliged to float well over a hundred miles

before we again came to land; after the lapse of three days we
got to see the spires and towers of Amsterdam, toward which
we forthwith sailed, and early the fourth day at ten o'clock
we landed there with our plank behind the burgomaster's garden, after enduring much danger. Thereupon we walked through
the burgomaster's garden ever toward his house, my brother
the count had to carry the plank now, and I went ahead; as we
now unlatched the garden gate leading into the burgomaster's
courtyard, there stood the burgomaster right in the door of his
house and watched us come marching up. I shall not tell anyone with what amazement the man looked at us, for we looked
as wet as bathed mice, water was still running down the velvet
trousers of the count, as though someone were pouring from
a vat. Quickly however I related to the burgomaster in two or
three words quite nicely how we had suffered shipwreck, and had
to float so far before we came to land. The burgomaster who,
the devil take me, was a solid, fine man, had great sympathy
with us; he led us into his room and had a warm fire lit whereupon I and my brother the count had to step back of the stove
into the warm spot to dry ourselves again. Now as soon as the
warm stove had helped us a bit, the burgomaster began to ask
who we were. I immediately began to tell him quite nicely about
my birth and how it had happened that time with the rat.
Zounds! What a pair of eyes the man popped open as I told
him such things about the rat, hereafter he always kept his
little cap under his arm whenever he talked to me, and addressed
me as Right Honorable Sir. After this relation, the burgomaster was called out and remained out I suppose a good half hour
before he returned; I and my brother the count were very
hungry because we neither of us had devoured a bit in four
days, therefore because no one was in the room, we looked to
see if anything good might be in the burgomaster's warming
oven in the warm spot of the stove; the count felt inside and
dragged out, the devil take me, a big pot full of sauerkraut
which was probably intended for the servants. Zounds! We took
pity on the sauerkraut and wolfed it, the devil take me, clean
down. Not long after, I and my brother the count became terribly ill from wolfing such down without bread on an empty
stomach. Zounds! We began to throw up and, the devil take me,
regurgitated the burgomaster's warming oven abominably full,
so that the stench in the room was such that we ourselves could
hardly remain there. Hereupon the burgomaster came back into

the room, and, smelling such, he began to speak to me: "Right Honorable Sir, Your Excellence surely has scorched itself at the stove that it smells so." Zounds! How was I supposed to answer the aristocratic man quickly at this? I was quick to tell him forthwith in such a nice *manière* how we as a matter of fact had been hungry, had got hold of and wolfed down the pot in the warming oven, and how when the stuff had not agreed with us, we had had to throw it up from us again, and that would be the reason for the present evil odor. Zounds! How the man listened that I could present such in such an adept *manière;* he thereupon calls his housemaid to clean out the warming oven and smoke the room a bit. This being done, he immediately had the table decked and treated me and the count, the devil take me, with right delicate foods. Now as soon as we had dined, some of the most aristocratic dignitaries came to the burgomaster's house and payed me and my brother the count a *visite.* They also invited us to their homes and tendered us great honor so that I may well say Amsterdam is, the devil take me, an excellent city. Right then there was an aristocratic wedding to which they likewise invited me and the count. For a London lord from England was marrying the daughter of an aristocratic dignitary in Amsterdam, and as it is now customary there for the aristocratic persons of quality invited to the wedding always to have a wedding *carmen* printed in honor of the bride and bridegroom and to present them with this, I too wanted to show that I was a fine fellow in this respect. It was just at the time when good midwife Gertraute felt that the flapping stork should soon turn up again, and since the bride's name was Traute, I would fain take my *invention* from the flapping stork, and the title should read:

The Merry Flapping Stork, etc.

I was quick to sit down with this project and sat well over four hours without hitting upon one line. The devil take me, I couldn't produce one word appropriate for the merry flapping stork; I bade my brother the count try to see if he couldn't produce something by way of emergency since I could hit upon nothing. Now the count said he had recently gone to school where he had learned a bit of poetasting, but he didn't know whether he was still competent, yet he would have a try whether he was. Hereupon the count sat him down, took quill and ink and began to poetize; what he then scribbled, were the following lines:

> In the heavens the lark itself already has presented,
> And gradually Mother Flora climbs from her nest;
> Yet in her room sleeps Maja firm forthwith and best,
> At present little joy is felt or intended.
> So will however . . .

When now he had sat with these lines a half hour I suppose, I peeped over his shoulder at the paper and saw what he had done; as I now read the stuff I was obliged, the devil take me, to laugh at my brother the count for such a silly concoction. For instead of using the flapping stork as he was supposed to, he had scribbled lark, and in place of Traute he had even used riot of bloom; is a riot of bloom appropriate for a wedding? And did it have rime topsy-turvey? For presented and nest rime, the devil take me, as well as a fist on an eye. He wanted to rack his brains with it some more, but I bade him let it be and sleep instead. Now although I couldn't concoct anything that day either, nevertheless I sat me down early the next day with it, and would fain make a *carmen* for the bride with Gertraute and the flapping stork. Zounds! As I touched the quill, what ideas about the flapping stork didn't I hit upon, so that, the devil take me, working with it no longer than half a day, it was done and ran thus as follows:

> The Merry Flapping Stork, etc., etc.
> Midwife Gertraude's day for us soon now shall ring,
> When the merry flapping stork us presents will bring,
> Over water and grass he will fly
> To bring our bride Traute a gift from the sky,
> The devil take me, she'll hold this so dear,
> And show it to none ere three-fourths of a year.
> To which end then wishes for this ceremony
> A body healthy and pert to eternity,
> A long life too, late and early,
> A person of quality
>                    Schelmuffsky.

Now as soon as the wedding days were approaching, I and my brother the count were requested by the father of the bride that we should do his daughter the great honor of conducting her to the wedding; whereupon I answered the wedding-father

very nicely, saying that for my part I should fain do this, but
I doubted very much whether my brother the count could be
present, because the rogue had got a cold fever and was con-
fined to his bed. The wedding-father was very sorry to hear
this, and since it couldn't be, the burgomaster in the meantime
had to take his place. When I now led the bride to the wedding,
zounds! What a gawking from the crowd, they practically
crushed one another, the devil take me, merely because each
wanted to see me so badly. For I walked along very nicely by
the bride in my black, long, silk cloak with a red, broad, velvet
collar. Now it is the mode in Amsterdam, that persons of quality wear pure red velvet collars on their black cloaks and high,
pointed hats; the devil take me, I can't say how nicely I conducted the female to the wedding and how *proprement* the
pointed hat and long cloak with the red velvet collar became me.
When now the wedding was over and the celebration began, I
was quickly obliged to seat me by the bride who sat in the
place of highest honor next to the bridegroom; not until then
did the other aristocratic persons of quality sit down; they all
gazed at me in the greatest amazement, especially those who
had not seen me in full, and they certainly thought to themselves that I must be one of the finest and most aristocratic
fellows in the world (which of course was true), since one
had conferred upon me the high place of honor. After we now
had thus dined for awhile, the master of ceremonies stepped
up to the table, stating that whoever of the persons of quality
among the wedding guests had composed a *carmen* honoring
the bride or bridegroom should now be so good to present it.
Zounds, how they all reached into the pockets of their great-
coats, each one bringing forth a printed paper and all of a will
to hand them over. But because they noticed me too fishing
around in my trousers, and likewise seeking something, they
thought forthwith that I too would have had something printed,
and no one would precede me. Finally I pulled out my *carmen*,
which I had had printed on red satin, from the lining of my
trousers. Zounds! How excited the people were, I now presented
this first of all to the bride with a completely nice *compliment*.
Seeing the title of it, zounds, what a face the female made, but
now after perusing it she twisted her eyes in her head, the devil
take me, like a calf, and I know that she surely thought, if only
the flapping stork were already there. The others now I suppose
got wind of the fact that my wedding *carmen* would have to be

the best of all, so, the devil take me, almost all put theirs back
into their trouser pockets. To be sure, some turned theirs in,
but neither bride nor bridegroom devoted to them one eye, but
forthwith placed them under a plate, but, the devil take me,
there was such a rush for mine because they all would fain see
and read it. Why? In the first place it was of uncommon *invention*, in the second place it was completely nice and charming
German. On the other hand the other persons of quality had
only used halting words and unrhymed German for their verses;
zounds, what an uproar was aroused among the people after
reading my *carmen;* they continually put their heads together
and kept watching me in the greatest amazement that I was
such a fine fellow, and they kept saying furtively to one another
that there must be something very important about me. Shortly afterward the bridegroom stood up and began to toast my
health. Zounds! How quickly the other persons of quality stood
up and made great reverences to me. But I remained seated
and looked at the whole line of them with such a nice countenance; the burgomaster, with whom I and my brother the count
were lodging, kept laughing so that his belly shook, he felt
such a cordial joy that everybody venerated me thusly. Why?
Because it was an honor for the man himself to have such an
aristocratic person like me occupy his house. My health now
having been toasted around the table, I had the master of ceremonies bring me a large water tankard holding, I suppose,
twenty-four tankards of the local measure; I bade a servant
fill this full of wine and hand to me across the table; the bridegroom, bride, and other wedding guests seeing this, they thereupon opened up their mouths and noses, not knowing what I
would do with the water tankard there on the table.
But I was quick to stand up in a nice *manière*, held the tankard
of wine in my hand and said: "Long live Traute the bride."
Zounds, how the other persons of quality all bowed toward me.
Whereupon I put the water tankard to my mouth and gulped
the twenty-four measures of wine clean down in one draught
and hurled it against the tile stove so that the pieces flew about.
Zounds, how they looked at me, if before they hadn't been
amazed at me when they were reading my wedding verses, now
they really were astounded to see how I could gulp down the
water tankard full of wine so nicely. Forthwith I had the servant fill me another such tankard full of wine and hand to me
across the table; like the first one I now gulped this down to

the bridegroom's health (his name was Toffel). Zounds! How
the dignitaries' daughters, sitting at the other table, all stretched
their necks up to me; the females were terribly astounded at
me, the devil take me, when they saw that I could drink so
nicely. Shortly thereafter, such an unexpected and rapid sleep
befell me that I couldn't resist laying my head on the table to
listen a bit. Seeing this, the bride bade me lie awhile on her lap,
for the table was way too hard, which I did without hesitation.
However I couldn't lie long on her lap, for it was too low for
me, my head began to ache from this, and I was quick to lay
me on the table again. Whereupon bridegroom Toffel ordered
a servant to bring me a cushion from the bride's chamber that
I might not lie there so hard. The servant quickly ran and
brought the cushion, the bride put it in the corner, saying I
should lay me thereon and slumber a little half hour; I was
quick to lay me full length on the bench behind the table; to be
sure an aristocratic woman of quality was sitting right near
me, she was obliged to slide far down that I might not soil her
dress with my feet.

Lying now for about half of a quarter hour, zounds, how
sick I became and began to groan. The bride, devoted to me
above the others, wants to see after me and inquire what my
trouble is, but she doesn't perceive, nor do I, that I am so close
to throwing up, and there I began to spew, and the devil take
me, I spew the bride's bosom quite full, so that it kept on running through below. Zounds, what a stench was there, they
were all obliged to take notice and go away; the bride went out
forthwith to her room and was of a will to change clothing;
the wine had quite dulled my head, I therefore lay there and,
the devil take me, I could hardly recollect where I was. The
other persons of quality noticing that I am full, they have me
taken to my quarters to sleep off the intoxication. Awakening
again the following morning I didn't know, the devil take me,
what I had done the previous evening; I gathered I was so full
because people were saying in the street that the aristocratic
foreign gentleman could drink so well and had thrown up so
terribly, from which I presumed that I must have drunk too
much. It now being time again for the noon meal, the master
of ceremonies came and bade me come right soon to the wedding
house, for they were all waiting for me with the bridal soup.
I was quick forthwith to put myself in order again and sent
word by the master of ceremonies that they should only delay

the meal a little half hour, I would come right away. But shortly thereafter the bridal carriage with four horses came and
fetched me from the burgomaster's house. As soon as I came
driving up to the wedding house, bridegroom Toffel was standing in the door with his bride to receive me; likewise they
opened the bridal carriage for me to climb out, which I proceeded to do and forthwith leaped out with both feet over
bridegroom Toffel, which was right nice to behold, whereupon
they led me into the room. Zounds, what great reverences all
the persons of quality made to me. Forthwith I was obliged to
sit by the bride again, and next to me on the left sat a dignitary's daughter; she too, the devil take me, was a nice girl,
for this day they had seated the ladies and gentlemen alternate-
ly. Now I didn't know I had thrown up into the bride's bosom
yesterday, but Toffel, her bridegroom, told me, and inquired
whether I felt better today after yesterday's regurgitation.
Zounds, how terrified was I to hear that I had caused such a
shameful scene at table yesterday. But hereupon answering
Toffel, that was the bridegroom, very nicely, I said that I was
a fine fellow, few of the like of whom one would find, and that
I had committed a *faux pas* by spewing the bride's bosom full,
it had happened during intoxication, and I hoped that by now
she would have had her things washed clean again. Did anyone
dare to say a word hereupon? The burgomaster knew all right
how things stood with me, and that no one would presume to
insult me with impunity; he now kept laughing so that his belly
might have burst. Finally I thought, you must tell marvelous
things again that they may really open up their mouths and
noses and regard you solidly. Forthwith I was quick to begin
to relate my marvelous birth and the incident of the rat.
Zounds, how the people at the table all looked at me, and especially Toffel the bridegroom. The dignitary's daughter sitting
by me appeared, the devil take me, not a hair different to me
from my drowned *Charmante;* she whispered probably ten
times over the table into my ear, saying I should tell the rat
story once more, and wanted to know whether the hole was
really big into which it had run after devouring the silken
dress. Likewise she indicated an interest in marriage to me, and
inquired whether I would take her, her father should forthwith
endow her with twenty thousand ducatoons, not to mention the
personal possessions which she still had, inherited from her
mother. Whereupon answering her very nicely, I said that I was

a fine fellow who had already tried his hand at some important
things in the world, and who likewise wanted to try further.
Thus I could not forthwith come to a decision, but should have
to consider a bit. While I was conversing with the dignitary's
daughter, Mr. Toffel, the bridegroom, began to inquire why I
had not brought along the count? Whereupon I answered ver ·
nicely, saying that because he had the common fever and couiu
not stay up, they would have to excuse him this time for being
unable to be a wedding guest. Whereupon the noon meal now
being ended, the dancing began; zounds, how *galamment*
the girls dance in Holland, they place their feet, the devil take
me, so nicely, it is an art. Now I too was obliged to dance, as
a matter of fact with the dignitary's daughter who had sat at
my left at table and spoken of marriage to me. Now at first
they just danced ordinary dances as *sarabandes, chiques, ballets,*
and such. I went along with all that now. Zounds, how they
all looked at my feet because I could place them so nicely. After we had now thus hopped about a good while, a quite nice
circle dance was arranged by the cavaliers and their ladies
which I also was obliged to dance. The idea was this: The
cavaliers or young bachelors had to form a circle, and each
man in the circle had to have a lady stand on his shoulders and
cover his face with her skirt so that he couldn't see; this done,
the music to the dance of death began, and the young bachelors
had to dance accordingly. Zounds, how *propre* was the dance.
Now I had the dignitary's daughter, who had fallen in love
with me, standing on my shoulders and danced very nicely with
her around in the circle. Zounds, the female was so heavy that,
the devil take me, I grew quite tired on this account, yet no
cavalier dared to stop dancing until his lady had fallen down.
This circle dance now ended, they all begged me to dance solo.
Now I could easily grant them the favor of dancing solo. I was
quick to give the musicians two ducatoons, saying: "*Allons,*
gentlemen, how about playing the Leipzig ditty once?" Zounds,
how the fellows began to scrape their fiddles. Whereupon I now
began just with cross capers and leaped up, the devil take me,
several fathoms high so that the people concluded surely that
something was going to spring out of me. Zounds, how people
came running in to the wedding house from the street, they
were watching me there in amazement. Having now danced off
the Leipzig ditty, I was now obliged, with this same dignitary's
daughter, who would become my dearest, to stroll about the city

of Amsterdam a little in order to cool me off a bit. I fell in with
this proposal and walked around a little in the city with this
female because I hadn't really got a good look at her yet. Now
she led me all around, wherever there was something to see. I
was likewise obliged to accompany her to the Amsterdam Stock
Exchange which, the devil take me, is built *proprement*. Here
she likewise showed me the tombstone of deceased Admiral
Reyter established as a perpetual memorial because Reyter was
such an excellent hero at sea and is always still very much
mourned in Amsterdam. The dignitary's daughter having now
shown me this and that, she said, turning to me, that I really
should take her and that if I should fain not remain in Amsterdam with her, then she would pack her bundle and wander off
with me wherever I wished, even though her father should
know nothing thereof. Whereupon answering her, I said I was
the finest fellow in the world, it might work out, but couldn't
be arranged so quickly, I would surely consider ways and
means and report to her soon. Whereupon I returned to the
dancing place to see where my future dearest might be who had
run away from me so fast on the street; I wore my eyes out
looking for her, but couldn't get to see her. Finally an old
woman began to address me, saying: "Your Grace, whom are
you looking for?" Answering her now, I asked whether she
had not seen the female who had sat on my left at table. "Yes,
Your Grace," the old woman continued, "I saw her, however
her father ordered her home and gave her a terrible scolding
for succumbing to the great boldness of permitting such an
aristocratic gentleman to conduct her around the city so that
people would now have something to gossip about, and Your
Grace wouldn't take her anyway." The old mother having thus
informed me, I inquired further whether she might not return
soon. Whereupon she answered me by stating that she doubted
her return here very much, for her father (as she had heard)
had told her: "Stubborn girl, don't show yourself again to the
aristocratic gentleman." Zounds, how such business vexed me,
that I should not get to see the female, and when she really
didn't return, I presented my wedding gift to Mr. Toffel, the
bridegroom, as well as to bride Traute, and took a quite nice
leave of them, as well as of the other persons of quality and
ladies, and kept on towards the burgomaster's house. The same
day they now sent the bridal carriage with four horses twenty
to thirty times again, begging me please to present my aristo-

cratic person at the celebration just this one evening still, even though I shouldn't desire to return for the other days. But the devil take me, I didn't return, but kept sending the bridal carriage back to the wedding house empty again. Mr. Toffel, the bridegroom, informed me by the burgomaster, he should not hope that one of the wedding guests would have offended me and that I should just let him know what was wrong with me. He would be responsible for everything. However, the devil take me, no one, except the old woman, learned what my trouble was, that I was so angry on account of the dignitary's daughter whom I should not get to see again. I was also of a will forthwith to sail again the same day, if my brother the count had not begged me so sorely not to leave him in his indisposition, but to delay until he had thrown off his fever again, after which he would travel with me wherever I wished. So to favor my brother the count, I stayed in Amsterdam two whole years still, spending my time mostly in gambling houses where every day there was always excellent company of aristocratic ladies and cavaliers. The elemental fever now having left my brother the count completely, I went with him to the *banco*, we drew new bills of exchange, and, boarding a ship, were of a will to have a look at India in which country the Great Mogul resides.

# The Fifth Chapter

The dog days appeared in the calendar the very day that I and my brother the count took leave of the burgomaster in Amsterdam and set us upon a big warship. We had been sailing about three weeks at sea on our way to India when we came to a place where terribly many whales were swimming in the water; these I enticed quite nigh our ship with a bit of bread. A sailor had fishing tackle with him, he had to give me this, and I tried to hook one onto the ship; the devil take me, I should have succeeded if the tackle had not broken to pieces, for when the whale first bit and I was just pulling fine, the crap broke in two, so that the hook stayed in the whale's maw, whereof without fail he will have died. Observing such and merely the shadow of the hookline, the other whales all swam away and, the devil take me, not a single one showed himself again at our ship. We sailed farther on from here and after some days got to see the Curdled Sea, where we had to sail past quite nigh. Zounds, what ships were standing there in the Curdled Sea, it was exactly like looking into a great barren forest where trees stood withered, and no soul was to be seen on the ships. I asked the captain how it was that so many ships stood there. He answered me, saying that the wind had driven these ships hither in a great storm, that the sailors had been bound for India, but had lost their way, and that consequently everybody on the ships had had to perish pitiably. Having now passed the Curdled Sea, we sailed under the equator. Zounds, what a heat was there. The sun soon burned us all pitchblack. Now my brother the count, a corpulent, fat gentleman, he became sick from the cruel heat under the equator, lay him down and died, the devil take me, before we were aware of it. Zounds, this affected me deeply that the fellow was obliged to die there and was my best traveling companion. But what could I do? Dead he was, and no matter how sorely I should have mourned him, I should not have got him back anyway. However I was quick to bind him to a plank according to ship custom, stuck two ducatoons into his black velvet trousers, and sent him away therewith onto the water; where he may now lie buried, the devil take me, that I can't tell anyone. Three weeks after his death we arrived with a good wind in India, where we debarked at a beautiful, blooming mead, settled our passage with the captain, whereupon one betook himself this way, someone else

another way. I forthwith inquired where the Great Mogul resided; first I asked a little boy who was running around there
with a little green cape on the same blooming mead where we
had landed and was herding young geese. Him I addressed right
nicely, saying: "Listen, little boy, can you inform me where the
Great Mogul of this land dwells?" The boy however couldn't
even talk yet, but only pointed with his finger, saying "a a."
Now the devil take me, I knew not what a a should mean. I
walked on farther across the mead and a scissors grinder drove
up to me, him I now also asked whether he could impart to me
information concerning where the Mogul must live. Whereupon
the scissors grinder forthwith informed me, explaining that two
Moguls resided in India, one they called the Great Mogul, but
the other only Little Mogul. Hearing now that I would to the
Great Mogul, he told me forthwith that it was about an hour
still to his residence, and that I should just continue on the
blooming mead, I couldn't go wrong; when this ended I should
come to a big city wall, I should just walk round the rear of
this circular wall, it would lead me to the castle gate where the
Great Mogul resided, for his residence was called Agra. The
scissors grinder now having imparted this information to me,
I continued on the blooming mead and on the way recalled the
little boy in the green cape who said a a; I was quite convinced
that the little rascal, even though he couldn't talk much, must
have understood me after all and known where the Great
Mogul dwelt, although he couldn't yet pronounce Agra but merely babbled a a. The scissors grinder's information hit the nail
on the head, the devil take me, for as soon as the blooming mead
petered out, I came to a big circular wall behind which I
marched forth, and as soon as this ended, I came to a terribly
big gateway before which stood well over two hundred satellites
with bared swords; they all had on green baggy trousers and
leather collars with roast pig sleeves. I forthwith got the idea
that the Great Mogul would reside therein. I was quick to ask
the satellites if their master were at home, whereupon the fel
lows all shrieked yes at once and would know my business.
Forthwith I now told the satellites that as a matter of fact I
was a fine fellow who had tried his hand at some important
things in the world and who wanted to try further, they should
just announce to the Great Mogul that I was so and so and that
I would fain have a few words with him. Zounds, how fast hereupon twelve of them ran to the Great Mogul's room and an-

nounced me to him. But they soon came running out again, saying I should walk in, their master would be very pleased that someone from a foreign country would honor him by paying a call. Whereupon I passed through the watch. I had hardly taken six steps before the Great Mogul cried out from his chamber upstairs that they should present arms before me. Zounds, hearing this, the fellows leaped to their guns and all held their hats under their arms and looked at me with the greatest astonishment. For now I could pass through the watch right nicely so that, the devil take me, it aroused great excitement with the Great Mogul. Having now come to a great marble stairs where I should ascend, the devil take me, the Great Mogul came a good half way down the stairs to meet me, receiving and conducting me by the arm all the way up. Zounds, what a beautiful hall was presented there, it flickered and flared with pure gold and jewels, the devil take me. In this very hall he now welcomed me, was pleased to hear of my good health, and said that he had not had the good fortune for a long time to have a German call upon him, whereupon he inquired concerning my position and origin, and who I was. Whereupon I now related to him forthwith very nicely my birth and the incident of the rat, and how I was one of the finest fellows in the world who had already seen and endured so much. Zounds, hearing me tell these things, how the Great Mogul listened. After such relation he forthwith conducted me into an excellently decked out room, saying that the same stood at my service and that I should stay with him as long as I would, it would please him and his wife very much. Forthwith he summoned pages and lackeys to serve me. Zounds, how the fellows came, what foolish reverences they made before me. First they bowed their heads down to the floor before me, then they turned their backs to me and at once scraped both feet far back. The Great Mogul commanded them to serve me correctly indeed, otherwise, should the most trifling complaint turn up, lackeys as well as pages should be led into the kitchen. Whereupon he took leave of me, returning to his room. Now when he was gone, zounds, how excellently the lads served me, to be sure they addressed me solely as junker, and whatever they could deduce from my eyes, that they executed. If occasionally I even expectorated, they all ran forthwith, the devil take me, to tramp it out, for whoever tramped out my expectoration first considered himself ever greatly honored. Hardly had the Great Mogul left me a half hour before he entered my room again with his wife, cavaliers, and *dames*. His wife as well as the cavaliers and *dames* all bade me now welcome and observed me in great amazement. At the request of the Great Mogul I was obliged to retell the incident of the rat, for his wife wanted sorely to hear this history. Zounds, how the female laughed thereat, the cavaliers and *dames* however looked at me in great amazement and kept saying furtively to one another that I must be very important in Germany since I could relate such things. It was now just time for dinner, the Great Mogul had the call to board sounded. Zounds, what a sounding and pounding of trumpets and military drums was heard. Two hundred trumpeters and ninety-nine military drummers stood in the courtyard of his castle on a great, broad stone; to honor me they had to let themselves be heard there; the devil take me, the fellows blew unforgetably. When now they had blown out, I had to take the Great Mogul's wife by the hand and escort her to the table, the devil take me, I looked right nice walking thus beside her. Arrived in the dining room, the Great Mogul insisted upon my sitting at the highest place of honor; I should have accepted this without hesitation too if I had not desired to sit by his wife, for that was such a wonderfully beautiful female. Accordingly the Great Mogul had to take his place first, I sat me down beside him, and by me on my left his dearest now sat, I was sitting right nicely there in the middle. All sorts of topics were now being discoursed upon at the table. The wife of the Great Mogul inquired of me whether good beer were brewed in Germany and which beer was considered the best. Whereupon answering her very nicely, I said that as a matter of fact good beer was brewed everywhere in Germany, and especially in the town where my home was; there people brewed beer which they just called sticky beer for the reason that it was so malt-rich that it completely stuck your fingers together and tasted as sweet as pure sugar, and that whoever had drunk even one measure of this same beer afterward could preach a sermon forthwith. Zounds, how amazed were all that Germany had such good beer with such strength in it. While we were now discoursing thusly at the table about this and that I would fain relate the tale of my pea-shooter; the Great Mogul's own songstress walked into the dining room, she had an Indian lyre hanging at her side. Zounds, how the female could sing and accompany herself thorough-bass on the lyre so artfully that my life long I had never heard anything in the world more beautiful, the devil take me. Can not say what a beautiful singing voice the female had. The devil take me, she could sing up as high as the nineteenth lined C, and reached a fifth trill as far as the octave two hundred beats long in one breath and didn't even get sour. In front of the table she sang an aria about red eyes and black cheeks which, the devil take me, was quite artful to hear. Dinner now being finished, I was again obliged to take the wife of the Great Mogul by the hand and escort her to my room where she, as well as the Great Mogul, cavaliers, and *dames* took leave of me, wishing me a good night, whereupon I thanked them very nicely and hoped that all should sleep very well and have pleasant dreams. Hereupon they all left my room and went likewise to lay them to bed. They now being departed, four lackeys and three pages entered my chamber, inquiring whether the junker would now undress. Now answering them that I was indeed sleepy and should not stay awake long, zounds, how busy were the fellows, one ran and fetched me a pair of quite golden slippers, another a beautiful night cap embroidered in gold, the third an incomparably beautiful sleeping fur, the fourth unbuckled my shoes, the fifth took off my stockings, the sixth brought me a quite golden chamber pot, and the seventh opened up the bed chamber for me. Zounds, what a beautiful bed stood there for me to sleep in, the devil take me, it was also so *propre* that I can't describe it enough; and it was likewise such soft sleeping therein that I didn't even awaken once the whole night. The same night I had a nice dream. For I dreamed that I wanted to take a beer-walk to the toilet and could not find same, and indeed I didn't find it either because now the previous evening at the table I had drunk a little strong, and joke and seriousness were confused; it seemed to me in the dream exactly as if one of the lackeys were carrying in a big silver tub, saying: "Junker here's something for you." Whereupon I clasped it and quite believed, the devil take me, that the tub would help me in my need, and it did help me in my need in the dream. Awakening early in the morning however, zounds, what kind of business had I transacted in my dream, the devil take me, I was almost floating in bed, it was so wet underneath me. Still it was good that I hadn't gone whole hog in the dream, I shouldn't have known in what manner such *faux pas* could be glossed over; anyway I remained lying a fine long time in bed and thus dried it out nicely underneath me again, so that no one noticed what

I had done. Whereupon I got up and had myself clad again;
when I was now finished, the Great Mogul sent to me, having
me greeted a good morning, and if I should have dreamed something pleasant, he should be pleased to hear it, likewise he
would like to trouble me to come to his privy *cabinet*. He should
like to consult me about a matter. Whereupon I was quick to
send word to him by way of answer, informing him very nicely
that I had slept very well, but that as to dreaming, I had had
no good dream, because a cold sweat had so oozed out from me
in a dream, but as to my joining him in his *cabinet*, the same
should ensue forthwith. I sent this word to him now by his
chamber page and thereupon went to him to hear what his request was. When I now came to him and had tendered my *compliments* very nicely to him, he unlocked a big bookcase and
fetched out a big book bound in pigskin; he showed same to me,
saying that he entered his income in this daily, and when the
year was over and he totaled up the *summa*, it would never
turn out right, the third part of his income was always lacking;
whereupon he inquired if I could reckon, to which I then replied to him that I was a fine fellow well acquainted with Adam
Riese's arithmetic book; he should give me the big book, I should
soon see how to make the *summa* balance. Hereupon he handed
me the book wherein stood his income and left me alone. As I
now leafed through the book, zounds, what fees and interest it
contained. I was quick to sit down, and taking quill and ink, I
began to count 1, 10, 100, 1,000, and when I now perceived that
the Great Mogul was lacking in one times one and didn't have
this in his head right, I saw indeed that it couldn't have been
otherwise that the sum of the third part came out less with
him than what he had written down daily: 10 x 100 is 1,000 but
he had calculated 10 x 1,000 is 100, and where he should have
subtracted, for example, one from 100 equals 99, he had subtracted thusly: one from 100 I can't do, one from 10 equals 9,
and 9 from 9 is zero. The devil take me, it's impossible for that
to balance. Now perceiving such errors, I noticed forthwith what
the trouble was. I was quick to sit down at this, and reckoned
hardly two hours before I balanced everything with the correct
sum, and had only half as much remainder from the whole that
he daily took in and entered. Having now made the calculation
very nicely and correctly from Adam Riese's arithmetic book,
I summoned him back to me and showed him one times one, and
that I had brought everything out so nicely and correctly with

only half as much remainder. Zounds! When I chattered of the remainder, he leaped up high for joy, clapped me on my shoulders, saying that if I were inclined to stay with him, he would make me his Privy Chancellor. Answering him hereupon, I said that there was indeed something about me, that I was one of the finest fellows in the world, and that because I had set my heart on seeing foreign countries and cities he should consider himself herewith thanked by me for the good offer. Now seeing that I had no desire for such a *charge*, he nevertheless tendered me such honor the whole fourteen days that I visited him, that, the devil take me, I shall never forget it as long as I live. For he is a terribly rich gentleman, the Great Mogul, he is addressed there only as Emperor, and has as many treasures as the year has days, I have seen them all too. For he showed me one every day. Excellent, beautiful books he has too, and is an especial connoisseur of same; I was obliged to promise by hand and mouth that, by way of return for money and good words, I would send him one from Germany for his bookcase. Now perceiving that I was readying myself for travel again, he honored me with his portrait with the chain, and his wife presented me with one thousand specie ducats of a type whereon the Great Mogul's portrait was struck. Herewith I hung the Great Mogul's portrait on me with the chain of the most beautiful Indian gold, and took leave very nicely from him, as well as from his wife, cavaliers, and *dames*, and went therefrom toward England by ship.

# The Sixth Chapter

After I had now taken leave of the Great Mogul, and he
had escorted me on foot up to the end of his city wall with his
entire retinue, I marched on the same blooming mead where I
had landed fourteen days before, ever toward the same water
again, and re-embarked on a big freighter which would sail to
England, and sailed away on same. On board I now related to
the captain very nicely too how the Great Mogul had entertained
me so excellently, and upon my departure had likewise honored
me with his portrait with the chain. I now thought the skipper
would gape big at this and be amazed at me for being such a
fine fellow; however, the devil take me, not in the least, the
fellow didn't even doff his hat for me, but rather began to tell
me that some people were more often lucky than right. Zounds,
how it vexed me to have the lazy lout chatter of such things,
and it wouldn't have taken much for me to give him a half dozen
blows. Yet I finally thought, he's a simple person, what can you
do with him, he doesn't know you or your position, let it therefore be at that. Afterward I told my comrades aboard of my
strange birth, as well as of the incident with the rat, and of my
pea-shooter. Having now sailed away three days and five nights
from the Indian blooming mead, we came with our ship to
the great Mediterranean Sea. Zounds! What sea monsters were
to be seen there, I suppose several thousand kept swimming
about our ship. I had my sole joy at that time with a little seal;
I lured it quite nigh up to our ship with a bit of bread so that
it acted quite friendly and wanted to play with me; because it
looked so nice, I quickly wanted to snatch it out of the sea into
the ship; however as I reached for the blackguard, the obstinate
toad bit me thoroughly through all five fingers, the devil take
me, and thereupon dived down. Zounds! How the blood ran
down among my fingers, they bled a good eight days before
stopping again, they pained me thoroughly after the bite. Finally the skipper brought me a little glass of olive oil, he bade me
grease my fingers therewith, saying that olive oil was so admirably good for a bite. I was quick to grease my fingers therewith; hardly two hours passed, before, the devil take me, everything was healed again. Having just about passed through the
Mediterranean Sea, terribly many sirens were visible in the
sea from afar; these females sing, the devil take me, admirably
beautifully. The skipper becoming aware of same, he bade us

all stuff up our ears firmly, for when they came closer, they
would so enchant us with their wonderfully beautiful singing,
that we should be unable to move from the spot. Zounds! Hearing this, how firmly I stuffed up my ears and bade the captain
sail away fast. After three days we came to the Baltic Sea,
there we likewise sailed several weeks before we passed through;
what pike there were in this same sea, the devil take me, I'm
unable to tell anyone; the sailors had a net along on the ship;
zounds, what kind of pike the fellows caught there. The devil
take me, they had tongues like big calves, and some six tankards
of fat stuck to the pikes' tongues. Some months hereafter, after
we had passed through various rivers, we arrived fortunately
in England where I got out at London, paid the skipper my passage, walked into the city of London, and took quarters with
the potter à la mode dwelling hard by the gate. Now the fellow
was finally very polite toward me, receiving me, and inquiring
what my wish was, whence I came, and who I was. Forthwith
I related to him very nicely my birth and about the rat and
how I was such a fine fellow and would fain take quarters with
him, likewise that I was inclined to stay incognito with him for
several weeks. This fellow, the potter à la mode, thereupon
could be talked to rightly, and likewise noticed in my eyes forthwith that I must be something important, but the rotter was
partially very indiscreet, for whenever he spoke with me, he
didn't always remove his hat, which then vexed me horribly at
him, that he did not pay me my due respect. I now thought,
good, I would deport myself in London merely as a poor cavalier and not appear as a person of quality; then, the devil take
me, the aristocratic London lord, Mr. Toffel, came walking into
the room of the potter à la mode with Traute, his dearest, at
whose wedding I had assisted in Amsterdam, and they bade me
welcome there. Zounds, how astonished I was that they had
forthwith ferreted me out. Hereupon they told me all; they
had seen me get off on the shore and slip into the house of the
potter à la mode so nicely, for Toffel, the aristocratic lord, had
his palace hard by in the same street. Whereupon he bade me
take quarters with him, but I had already lodged with the potter à la mode, and the man would fain not have me leave, and
I would not gladly change quarters, for it would only have
caused a to-do with the people if I had my things thus hauled
back and forth. That very evening I was invited to dine by Mr.
Toffel, the aristocratic lord, at whose house there were also

many other persons of quality and aristocratic daughters of
lords; they all fell in love with me and indicated marriage to
me, for I showed them the portrait with the chain of the Great
Mogul, and related how he had presented me therewith and entertained me excellently because I could do the calculation of
his income very nicely and correctly; that as a matter of fact
he had half as much more than he had taken in the year long.
Likewise I told that he had wanted to make me his Chancellor,
however not yet desiring to settle down, I had politely rejected
the good offer. Zounds, how the females, the aristocratic lords'
daughters, looked at me at the table, they all began to toast
my health. One said, long live the Chancellor of the Great Mogul
in India, the second said, long live the aristocratic foreign
gentleman who was presented with the Great Mogul's portrait,
the third said, long live in memory a high person of quality
whose eyes reveal some importance. Perceiving now that all
this was meant for me, I turned a very nice countenance toward
the ladies toasting my health so that it looked, the devil take
me, very nice. The story of the Great Mogul now being finished,
I began to chat somewhat of my strange birth and of the rat.
Zounds! How all the aristocratic lords, hearing these things,
opened up their mouths and noses. The following morning, the
dearest of Mr. Toffel arranged on my account the *tour à la
mode,* whereby to favor me over two hundred coaches of persons of quality and the most aristocratic lords' daughters accompanied me from London; I was obliged to sit in the carriage
with two of Mr. Toffel's maiden aunts. I can't tell, the devil
take me, how the females acted with me en route, they almost
devoured my mouth, so much did they embrace me. Now they
had me sitting between them, which was very nice to see, for
I had hung out my portrait from the coach; well over one
hundred lads were running after the carriage. After we now
about two miles from London came to the place where the
*tour à la mode* was being held, zounds, how excellently was I
entertained there, they likewise tendered me such honor at this
very place that, the devil take me, I can't tell it. The following
morning thereupon the maiden aunts of Mr. Toffel came driving
up in their coach to the house of the potter *à la mode* where
I had quarters and bade me, if I pleased, drive with them a
little, they would fain show me something of the antiquities of
the city of London which I probably had not yet seen. Whereupon without hesitation I sat me by them in the carriage, and

again in the middle, which was right nice to see. Now after we
had driven around a corner in London with Mr. Toffel's maiden
aunts, we came to a great chapel before which we got out and
all three went in there. Therein lay well over two hundred
three-score of scythes whereon the blood still stuck thick as a
finger. I now asked Mr. Toffel's maiden aunts what all the
scythes were doing there, and why so much blood was sticking
to them all, they answered me that they were preserved there
as rarities and shown to all foreign persons of quality, for the
soldiers of the Duke of Monmouth or whatever his name was
had all been likewise armed therewith, and they had sabred off
the heads of those people with such scythes in such a stately
manner. After this all three of us sat very nicely in our coach
again and drove to another place, where they likewise showed
me the stone on which the patriarch Jacob is supposed to have
eaten when he saw the ladder to Heaven in a dream. From
there we again drove forth and came to a place where hung a
great axe with which an aristocratic person's head had been
chopped off. They told me the name of the person too, but the
devil take me, I can't recall it any more. As they had now shown
me all this and that, we returned to Mr. Toffel's, with whom I
again dined. I must admit that throughout the three years I
was in London great honor was extended to me, the devil take
me, and especially by the aristocratic Lord Toffel and his maiden
aunts. As I now took leave of them to betake myself to the
Spanish Sea, the devil take me, the same females cried the bit-
terest tears for my leaving them, they begged me I suppose a
hundred times to stay by them, it shouldn't cost me a farthing.
Indeed, if I had done this, I suppose I should have remained a
fine fellow, however I hoped to climb ever higher by traveling;
this could easily have happened too, if I had not been so unlucky
on the Spanish Sea. In the following chapter you will soon hear
how I now fared there.

# The Seventh Chapter

If I am correct, it was the first or the last of April when I quite took leave of Mr. Toffel, the aristocratic London lord, together with his wife, Traute, as well as of his maiden aunts and the potter *à la mode*, who had been my innkeeper, and set myself upon a big freighter heavily laden with pike tongues and coming the same day from Portugal. On this I was now of a will to go to the country of Spain and sample the beautiful Spanish grapes there. We sailed forth from London very fortunately with good weather; on the Spanish Sea the wind was very *favorable* for us, and likewise the sky had thus cleared up that, the devil take me, you didn't see one little black flaw in the clouds; the captain now perceiving that the wind wished us so well, he bade as many of us, as were aboard, together to strike up a merry song, and likewise sang with us. While we were now thus in the best joy, I saw from afar a ship bearing down upon us which I showed to the captain and asked him what kind of a ship it might be. Viewing this, the captain forthwith began to tell us that it was flying strange flags and it appeared to him as if it might even be a pirate or caper ship. Zounds! My comrades hearing this, how terrified the fellows were; but I was quick to run down into the ship forthwith to see if all the pieces were ready; as I now blew into the muzzles of same to hear if they all stood loaded, the devil take me, not a single one was readied. What was to be done? I forthwith began to speak to my comrades; "*Allons*, gentlemen, the enemy is here! Let's keep our swords ready." Zounds! How the fellows stood there and trembled and shook, so terrified were they, when I chatted of swords and fighting. Hereupon it didn't last long before the pirate ship, on which was the famous pirate Hans Barth with terribly many pirates, sailed up to us like a stroke of lightning; he now asked forthwith whether we would surrender. But I answered him forthwith very nicely, saying: "I won't surrender, the devil take me." Zounds! How the fellow unsheathed with his pirates. Now I likewise wasn't slow to draw my excellent broadsword, which was a back scratcher, and go at the pirates. You could have seen some beautiful hewing and fencing there as I hewed into the fellows; the devil take me, I sabred off a piece of Hans Barth's big nose so that it flew far into the sea, and to this hour it can still be seen that he has a stub for a nose; I hewed and struck down I suppose about fif-

teen of the other pirates, without counting the others whom
I had hewn asunder and killed. But what could I do? If there
had not been so terribly many of the fellows against one man.
Indeed, if only my comrades at that time had only stood by me
a little, we should have won the *victoire* without fail. But the
lazy louts stood there with their fists shoved into their big coat
pockets and, the devil take me, kept letting themselves be hewn
at like cabbage and turnips, and didn't even make a move. The
devil take me, I was so crazed at the fellows, not even one of
the knaves would lift a hand, and you've always heard this:
Many dogs kill one rabbit. For Hans Barth had such a terrible
big following with him. Indeed, if there had only been about
twenty or thirty of them, I should soon have taken care of them,
but there were well nigh a hundred of the fellows who were all
over me, yet they themselves had to admit that something important had gleamed from my eyes when I had held them so
resolutely without receiving either a cut or a thrust. When now
I was finally tired of fighting, and saw that there was no possi-
bility of achieving *victoire,* the devil take me, I had to begin to
ask for *pardon.* There you could have seen some nice plundering
as the fellows came onto our ship. The devil take me, they took
everything we had from us. I began to tell them of my birth and
the incident of the rat, but the devil take me, they wouldn't
even believe it, but undressed us all down to our shirts, took
everything we had, and took us prisoner with them to St. Malo,
where they stuck each of us alone in a hideous prison. Zounds!
How I thought then of my previous position, who I had been,
and who I now was in the hideous hole. The Great Mogul's portrait with the chain was gone, the thousand specie ducats which
his dearest had presented me were gone, my other good money
along with the ducatoons I had drawn at the bank in Amsterdam were gone, my beautiful outfit, adorned with gold and silver in which the person of quality Schelmuffsky had deported
himself very nicely almost in the whole world, was gone. My
strange birth lay there in the dirt, no one would believe me that
the story of the rat had taken place, therefore like the most
miserable lazy lout in the world I had to lie there an innocent
prisoner in a hideous prison a whole half year! Zounds! How
miserable I was there, the devil take me, there were lice in the
devilish nest, one was as big as the rat which had devoured the
silk dress of my mother. The devil take me, they gave me no
peace either day or night; if now the whole day long I snapped

to death several thousand of them, by night about ten other
regiments took their place again, and at times my shirt was so
completely covered, that no single little speck of white could be
seen thereon. I often thought there of my previous position and
of London Lord Toffel's maiden aunts, that the females cried
about me so when I wouldn't stay by them. Yes, who can know
everything, and the devil take me, I should have rather fore-
seen otherwise than that it should happen like this to me. The
jailer at St. Malo likewise treated me very badly in prison, for
he never sent me anything but a quite big bowl full of clay
broth by his daughter whose name was Clauditte, I always
had to get along therewith three days before I got anything
again. Sometimes they even forgot me completely too, and only
brought me something again the sixth day, so that, the devil
take me, I often had to go hungry three days. Shortly before
the jailer announced my ransom at one hundred thaler, a ghost
appeared to me in prison: zounds! Seeing the spook, how I began to shriek. However the ghost, addressing me very nicely,
said: "Charming youth, you will soon attain your freedom
again, just be patient a little longer still." Hearing these words,
I didn't know, the devil take me, whether I was a girl or boy;
in part I was terrified, in part I was happy thereover because
it was chatting about charming youth and freedom. I was quick
to take heart and ask the ghost who it was. Answering me very
nicely, it said it was the spirit of *Charmante* my former dearest
who had had to drown on the ship near Bornholm with six
thousand souls. Now hearing this, that everything fitted to a T,
I was no longer terrified of the ghost, but would fain ask i'
further, whither *Charmante* had come when she drowned at
that time and where she lay buried. However, as I was thus
asking, the ghost, the devil take me, had forthwith disappeared
again. Hereupon it didn't last a half hour before the jailer came
to the front of my prison and said that if I could get hold of
one hundred thaler, he had orders to release me again. I answered him that I had been a fine fellow indeed who formerly
would have thought nothing of so much money, but now he
could well see that I was the most miserable lazy lout. The jailer
inquired further from what country and whence I came, and
if I possibly could make arrangements, then I could forthwith
write thither and describe my condition to my family. I now
related that I had a mother and was her only dear son, that
she had a very good competence, that she wouldn't begrudge so

much money when she heard that her dearest son was so miserable in a strange land. Hearing this, the jailer began to tell me that if I would write my Mother for so much money, I should be let out of the prison, and should be under *arrest* in his house only until the ship with the money should arrive. As soon as I had acquiesced in his wish he began with: "Open, you fetters and chains, and let the prisoner pass." Whereupon he took me to his house until the ship with the hundred thaler came sailing up. Having received the ransom, he honored me with a pair of old sailor's trousers, an old sailor's cap, a pair of old, disreputable stockings, likewise shoes, and an old pirate's cloak for the trip and let me wander forth therewith.

# The Eighth Chapter

Now the devil take me, I didn't know then whither I should march; I had not one bloody farthing to my name, I walked as the most miserable beggar, no one saw anything important in me anymore, and for the life of me I had no idea how I would come away again from St. Malo. Finally I went to where the ships sailed off, there I told a skipper my misfortune and how I had fared, and begged him please to take me along when he sailed, I should gladly lend him a hand aboard. The captain consented, for he was an English skipper and had fetched beautiful wares in France; he finally took pity on me and took me along; now, whenever a storm came and the waves thereof beat into the ship, I always had to pump so that the valuable things might not become wet, thus I got eating and drinking from him. Now sailing by London again, I said to the skipper that pumping was getting sour for me, and I could not possibly stand it any longer; I begged him please to let me get out there, I would fain make my way to the city. The skipper did not oppose me herein either, but sailed to the shore with his ship, let me go my way, and sailed forth from there. I was quick to sit down there by the water, pulled off my shoes, bound them together, hung them on my arm, and marched half barefoot in my ragged stockings ever towards the gate of the city of London. Having now come thereto, I stood still and considered a good while where I would set up my quarters there, because I didn't have a farthing of money. At first I was of a will to put up with the potter *à la mode* again; but I thought, what will the man ever and eternally think if the person of quality who deported himself so very well there a half a year ago now comes thus marching up like the most miserable tramp? Thereafter I was also of a will to put up by Mr. Toffel, the aristocratic lord, but, I thought too, if his maiden aunts would hear that I had returned from Spain so miserable, they would not only not rue me it, but thereto they would also have a really good laugh at me for not previously staying by them. Finally I resolved to retreat forthwith and lodge in the suburb at the beggars' hostel, where I met beggars whom I had shown very much goodness to by some alms a half year ago; some also told me that my face was familiar to them, and they should have seen me somewhere before; however they could no longer remember where. A little beggar boy began to say that I almost looked like the aristo-

cratic gentleman who a half year ago in London had always
hung out from the coach a piece of gold with a chain, which so
many three-score of boys continually had run after, thus to see
the piece of gold. However I didn't let on that it was I, and even
if I had told them forthwith, the devil take me, they would not
even have believed me.

The next day, because I had no money, I was quick to walk
into the city of London, there I asked people, who previously
hadn't seen me as a person of quality, for a penny for
subsistence; the devil take me, I didn't go to the places where
formerly I had often been a guest, for they could easily have
recognized me; and whenever I walked past Mr. Toffel's house,
I always pulled my cap over my eyes so that no one should
know me. By chance I also met a half countryman in London
who was a fine fellow who had proved brave in war;
him I told my misfortune, he honored me with a thaler and
promised to take me along back home free; but I had forgotten
the place where I should ask for him, and from the time when
he had given me the thaler I couldn't find it again. Two days
immediately afterward, to my great luck, three freight wagons
were driving from London to Hamburg; I asked the carters to
take me along, I should not consume much. The carters were
quite kind, saying that if I watched their wagons at night for
them they would take me with free board to Hamburg. Zounds!
Who was merrier than I, I said I should fain heartily do it.
Hereupon they now took me along and I had to sit forward on
the driver's seat and drive; when we now came to evening quarters, they always gave me the head or tail of a herring, and
thereto a big piece of bread; I now had to work this into me,
thereafter they also poured me a drink thereto and bade me lie
under their wagons and watch. Now that lasted night after
night, until we came to the last inn near Hamburg, where I
took leave of the carters. To be sure they asked if I wouldn't
go all the way to Hamburg; I thanked them no, yet I should
have liked to be therein, but I stood in fear that someone might
still recognize me there, and thereafter tell the watch that I
was so and so who several years ago had cut down and knocked
over so many of them. Thus I didn't dare, but marched up a-
round the next village before Hamburg, went up in open country so long until I came into another district where I was right
safe from the watch. Hereafter I begged my way from village
to village until I finally saw Schelmerode again and there, after

the very dangerous trip which I had survived on land as well as at sea, I greeted my Mother again pert and sound. The joys with which the honorable woman welcomed me at that time I shall likewise disclose in the future in the introduction of the Second Part very nicely.

For the present however the First Part
of my veritable, curious, and very
dangerous travel account
on sea and land is
ended.

# Schelmuffskys

curiöser
und
sehr gefährlicher

# Reise-Beschreibung

Zu Wasser und Lande

## Anderer Theil.

---

Gedruckt zu Padua eine halbe Stunde
von Rom/
Bey Peter Martau/
1 6 9 7.

# Schelmuffsky's

curious

and

very dangerous

# Travel Account
## By Sea and Land

## Second Part

---

Printed at Padua a half hour from Rome / At Peter Martau's /
1697

The robber Barth, with pirates his, may now brag,
How he on wild wave, swag much did snag,
However he will not by far the fame receive
Which Schelmuffsky by travel did it achieve.


The former ship comrade of Schelmuffsky at the herring catch before Rome on the Tiber wrote this in a towboat with the fastest quill in eternal memory. X. Y. Z.

# To the Ever Curious Reader.

To be sure I should have cause enough to keep the Second Part of my curious Travel Account under the bench and not publish it at all, and the devil take me, I could likewise do this in good conscience; however in the First Part, I opened up everybody's mouth with the promise of putting the Second Part together as soon as possible, because I would not make a pocket of my mouth, but would fain show the ever curious reader in several ways that I was one of the finest fellows in the world, even though I'm not that any more. If now the Second Part of my curious Travel Account, likewise the First, is diligently read by all with the greatest astonishment and everything therein believed, then I assure each person that next year, if I don't die, I shall likewise write something correct about my here and there forgotten trip, as well as of other memorable things, and publish the same under the title: Curious Months. Such things shall be put together which, the devil take me, no one can easily shake out of his sleeve. Meanwhile may the curious reader ever be well disposed toward that one who his life long will call himself

the ever curious reader's
most travel-desirous
SIGNOR Schelmuffsky.

# The First Chapter

If I remember rightly it was just on St. George's day when returning from my very dangerous trip in an old, mangled pirate cloak and indeed barefoot, I first again saw honest Schelmerode. Now the devil take me, I can't say how everything in the city of my birth appeared so strange and unfamiliar to me; likewise I had forgotten it so as if I had not looked at it my life long. Three whole days and nights I ran around on all the streets as a delirious person, and didn't know how to find my Mother's house again, even if it should have cost my life. If I asked people right away whether they couldn't inform me or at least only tell me the street where my Mother might dwell, they always gaped, the devil take me, looked at me, and laughed. To be sure, I couldn't be vexed at them for acting so stupidly and giving me no answers to my questions. Why? While abroad I had completely forgotten how to speak my Mother's tongue, for I gabbled mostly English and Dutch, occasionally German, and if you didn't pay close attention to my mouth, the devil take me, you couldn't understand a syllable. I believe I probably shouldn't have yet found my Mother's house in eight days, if the third night, between eleven and twelve, my maiden aunts hadn't by chance come upon me on the street, whom I likewise addressed and asked whether they couldn't give me information concerning my Mother's house. The females both looked sharply at my face in the dark and did not understand (although I was speaking very un-German) what I would have. Finally one began to speak, saying I should first identify myself, who I was, then they themselves would take me to the desired place. As I now related to them that I was so and so and that I had already run about the city three days and that no hangman would have been able to report to me in which street my Mother did live, zounds, how the females both fell on my neck in the street and were joyed at my good health and fortunate return. They both grabbed hold of my bedraggled pirate cloak and were of a will to march with me to my Mother's house. While now all three of us were walking along very nicely, and I began to tell them en route of my imprisonment at St. Malo, two fellows sneaked up behind me unnoticed; they think I am probably a journeyman because I walked so slovenly, and each one gave me there a blow from the rear so that forthwith red soup shot out of my mouth and nose as thick as a leg, whereupon they snatched my maiden aunts aside, and kept wandering with them, what's your hurry, what's the matter, as much as I could see in the dark, through a narrow little street. Zounds, how this business of such foolish fellows vexed me, because they did not respect me better. Their biggest luck was, that Hans Barth had stolen my excellent back scratcher on the Spanish Sea, otherwise I wouldn't have given a three-pence for their whole lives. However I thus had nothing in my fists, and it doesn't always work to take on affairs in the dark without a sword; therefore I thought, you'd better swallow the blows and wait until your maiden aunts come back, they'll surely tell you who the fellows were, thereafter they will have to give you *satisfaction* for the insult all right. I stood at the same place I suppose over three hours where I had received the blows, and waited for my maiden aunts.

When they now returned, they were quite full of joy, and related to me how they had fared so well, and how the same fellows who had delivered the blows to me had so excellently given them presents and they were very sorry because I was their cousin, that they had attacked me. Having now heard such from my maiden aunts, that it was all a mistake, and that the blows which I had received had been intended for someone else, I let it be and thought: to err is human. Whereafter my maiden aunts continued leading me to my Mother's house. Arrived now at the door, we couldn't come in. I suppose we knocked over four hours at my Mother's house, but no one would hear us. Perceiving now that no one would open to us, all three of us lay down supine in front of the door and slumbered there until the house was opened again; hereafter we slipped in furtively, went softly up the stairs to the chamber of my maiden aunts, so that no one noticed us. Upstairs, my maiden aunts now undressed, and put on their night gowns to the end that no one should notice that they had got some fresh air elsewhere last night. This having taken place, they bade me softy slip down the stairs again to rap at the door to my Mother's room and hear whether she would still know me. Coming now downstairs in the house again, zounds, how strange and unfamiliar everything seemed to me. I searched I suppose over two hours before I could find the door of my Mother's room again; for I had almost completely forgotten everything in the house, with the exception of my Mother's little dog, which she always took to bed with her and which afterward had to die an unexpected death; I still recognized same by its tail, for it had a

blue mark under its tail which I had unintentionally given it with
my pea-shooter a little while ago when I was going to school, and
had shot at a sparrow and unexpectedly hit the dog under the
tail. But when I saw my Mother she seemed, the devil take me,
quite unfamiliar to me, and I should never have believed that she
was my Mother either if I had not recognized her by the silken
dress which the big rat had previously chewed out; for therein
front and back was a horribly big hole, and to her good luck she
had just put on the chewed dress that very day, otherwise I
should not have recognized her, the devil take me.

After I now knew for certain, and the chewed silken dress
gave me sufficiently to understand, that I again saw my Mother
standing before me whom I had seen with no eye in so many
countless years, I thereupon identified myself, saying that I
was her son who had seen and experienced something of note in
the world. Zounds! How the female opened up a pair of eyes as
she heard that I should be her son Schelmuffsky. At first she said
the thing could not possibly be true, that I was her son, since her
son, as she had heard, was one of the most aristocratic persons
of quality under the sun and would, if he returned home, not
come dressed as slovenly as I. But hereupon I answered my
Mother very nicely, and helped her forthwith with two to three
words out of her dream, saying that to be sure I had been one of
the most aristocratic persons of quality in the world all right;
that a good apparel was of no use to you in traveling, and that
the Lord of Schelmuffsky had sat imprisoned a whole half year
in St. Malo, and that I was her only dear son, who on account of
a big rat and indeed according to Adam Riese's arithmetic
book, had come to the world four months too early. Zounds!
When my Mother heard of the rat, how the female fell on my
neck for joy and hugged and embraced me, that I can't say, the
devil take me. Having now fondled me a good while, she began
to cry for great joy so that the tears kept running down her
stockings and her chamois shoes became thoroughly soaked there
from. Hereto now came my maiden aunts walking into the room
in their night *habits* and offered my Mother a good morning, but
they acted towards me as if their life long they had not seen me.
My Mother at that time likewise had a little cousin with her, the
same was a sly toad, the creature was permitted to have his way
completely. While my Mother was now relating to her maiden
aunts that I was her son Schelmuffsky who had tried something

important in foreign countries and withstood much by sea and land, the little cousin must have heard that Schelmuffsky was being discussed in the room; the cheeky little know-it-all came leaping like a rat out of my Mother's bed and looked into the room. As soon as he now saw me, the little boy began, the devil take me, to laugh, and forthwith asked me what I would then want at home again since I had hardly been away fourteen days. Zounds, how this business of the boy about fourteen days vexed me. As now my Mother thereupon asked him if he knew me, the know-it-all answered her so scornfully, saying why shouldn't he then know his slovenly cousin Schelmuffsky. But when my Mother would open his eyes for him, saying that he must be seeing falsely, and that I had tried something important in foreign lands by sea as well as by land, my little cousin again began: "My aunt I hope will not be so naive to believe such lies; I've been told by various people that my cousin Schelmuffsky didn't get any farther than a half mile from the city of his birth, and drank everything up with slovenly company in tobacco and brandy." Zounds! How I gnashed my teeth as the boy rubbed tobacco and brandy under my nose. After this, my maiden aunts bade me really tell something of my dangerous trip, and what things I had seen in the world. As I now brought forth things which aroused great amazement with my maiden aunts, the boy kept interruping me, saying I should keep still, it was really all lies and fabrication, what I was bragging about there. Finally the louse got in my liver and, before he knew it, I gave him a blow that forthwith sent him flying against the door with his legs turned up high. Zounds, what an act my Mother put on on this account. How I thereafter fought and quarreled with my Mother on account of the boy; that couldn't be written, the devil take me, on any ass' skin, and in my opinion is unnecessary to make much fuss about. However if anyone is curious to have more precise intelligence about such business, I can't give any better advice than just to ask several honest wives in the neighborhood about this, the devil take me, they'll tell him minutely. However, in order to touch a little upon my condition at that time when I had returned from imprisonment, it will be described very nicely as follows.

# The Second Chapter

The first day of my arrival had hardly ended when I was quite
tired from quarreling with my Mother about my little cousin on
account of the delivered blow, and the house boy had to light my
way up to bed one hundred and eleven steps with a paper lantern. Hardly had I crept into the pig feathers when forthwith a
terribly sweet slumber overcame me, so that you could hear me
snore three houses away, and then I began to dream. Now, the
devil take me, it was a very meditative dream, for I dreamed I
was at sea, a horrible thirst seized me, but because I could find
nothing of the good drink with which I would quench my thirst,
it seemed exactly as if I took my pirate cap and filled this full
of sea water which was teeming with big, red worms and green
maggots; the devil take me, they had big, long, broad, and sharp
teeth in their snouts and stank like the foulest carrion; this same
water I now slurped into me with all these worms; it didn't taste
too bad, for the worms slipped down so smoothly that I didn't
even notice them, yet one was just about to catch in my throat,
if I hadn't swallowed in the dream, for he had caught with his
teeth on the plug under my tongue in my throat; however as soon
as I swallowed, he immediately joined the whole company.
After the elapse of a quarter hour you could hear a beautiful
screaming and howling in my stomach, zounds! How the worms
and maggots were biting one another in my body; the devil take
me, it was really a hare baiting, and they all were bleeding like
swine. Now after they had thus romped about a good while in
my body, I thereupon became atrociously ill and began to vomit;
then you could see some pretty puking, the devil take me; the
way I was vomiting, it poured forth front and back four whole
hours, and kept up into the bed during my dream, so that finally
as a consequence I woke up. Now awake, I lay, the devil take me,
up to my ears in pure filth, and well over one hundred thousand
such red sea worms and green maggots with big teeth were creep-
ing around therein; they were all gulping down the vomit again,
then disappeared before I knew it, and to this hour I don't know
whither they went; this vomiting now continued with me
four whole weeks night after night; it must have come from the
air, for I also broke out forthwith sorely on my hands and feet.
The devil take me, my whole body was completely like birch

bark, and my skin began to itch like nothing good; sometimes, when I had donned the pirate cape, I rubbed the leather so hard that the gleaming rubies in my pirate cape got stuck like paste or bookbinder's glue thick as your finger. I suppose it took me a good half year 'ere I could get this stuff out of my hair again; I shouldn't have been rid of it yet if I hadn't had a salve concocted of olive oil and broken bricks and had kept smearing my limbs diligently therewith. Ah, olive oil, olive oil, the devil take me, that's a splendid medicine against the itches. After I had now within the course of a year moulted, and could stand a little air again, no day then passed in which I wasn't obliged continuously to quarrel with my Mother; I was likewise so fed up with such a life as though I had devoured it with spoons; the row was generally due to my little cousin, because the lad was always so saucy and wouldn't believe any word I said. Finally when I saw that I couldn't get along with my Mother at all, I ordered her to have a new garment made for me and to give me my paternal inheritance in full, I would march again to foreign places and have a look at what was going on in Italy and France, perhaps I should have better luck there than on the Spanish Sea. Now my Mother would fain not hinder me in my undertaking, indeed, at that time she would rather have packed me off today than tomorrow. She had a nice, new garment made for me which was adorned with the most beautiful leonine piping; however, because she was not immediately flush with cash, and because she likewise had a claim to an inheritance in a neighboring city, she gave me an order for this by which I should have the money paid to me there in her name, so that she could thus get me out of her house again. Whereupon I was quick to hie me thither the same day, thinking that the monies would be counted out and waiting for me; however, when I got there, the debtor who was supposed to pay the money would not honor my order, but claimed I was not yet of age and furthermore he did not know whether I was so and so. Zounds, how vexing was this business, to be considered not of age in view of the fact that for countless years I had looked about in foreign lands far and wide and had been one of the finest fellows in the world. However I did just this, I related to him the incident of the rat and the hole into which it was supposed to have run. Zounds, how terrified the debtor then was of me and was, the devil take me, as ashamed as a dog. I believe he would have preferred to owe me half as much again than to have rubbed my not being of age under my nose. For he thereupon took a really good look at me for the first time, and when he noticed that something especial glistened from my eyes, he begged my pardon, and presented an excuse to the effect that he would fain pay me the inheritance, but at present he didn't have the means; in two years he would see to it that I should be helped. What would I now do, seeing that the good man didn't have it. However since I would not cause him detriment (for if I had complained, he would have had to pay me, and, the devil take me, with no good word), I was quick to transfer the entire inheritance to another person; I had him pay a fourth part of the whole rubbish, and assigned him power of attorney from my Mother to draw the entire capital. Having now received the money, zounds, who was merrier than I to have fresh pennies clinking in my trouser pocket again. As soon as I returned to my Mother's in Schelmerode, I again prepared to travel, packed all my things together in a large trunk, again in tears took leave of my Mother, as well as of my maiden aunts, and was of a will to take the fast post. When I now would wander out of the door with my big trunk, my little cousin approached me, I would now also wish him good night. However as I now offered him my hand, the little toad began to laugh, saying it would not be necessary for me to take leave of him, my trip would not be so extensive, and if he wanted to take the trouble to sneak after me, he would probably find me in the next village in a peasant pub, where I would remain long enough for the negotiated inheritance to be chased down my gullet in the form of tobacco and brandy, whereupon I would turn up again all right. Zounds! How this business with the boy vexed me, that he chattered on about such things in the next village. However I didn't hesitate, but again gave him unexpectedly such a blow, that a bright fire forthwith sprang out of his eyes, and hereupon without saying a word, marched out of the door with my big trunk, and with a full bound, what's your hurry, what's the matter, to the post house; now you could then have heard a pretty shouting after me from my Mother on the street as the female shouted and said: "Strike, you rogue, strike, and go and break your neck and leg and never appear before my eyes again." My little cousin, the saucy little rascal, pursued me with stones up to the post house, but he didn't even hit me once. When I now came to the post house, and the fast post was already quite full, the postillion would not take me along, yet he proposed that I should find a place behind on the luggage rack if I would come along. Whereupon I didn't long reflect, but forthwith jumped on with both legs together with my trunk and bade the postillion keep on driving out as fast as possible through the gate *per postae.*

# The Third Chapter

It was just the same day when the previous night my Mother's turkeys were stolen that I left the honest town of my birth and again for the second time set out upon my very dangerous trip by sea and land. We had hardly traveled a musket shot from the town when the postillion overturned us so that all four wheels of the post coach broke to pieces; the devil take me, the passengers which he was carrying lay up to their ears in the mud, for it was in an atrocious bog hole where he overturned us. I was very lucky to be sitting at the time back on the luggage box; for when I saw that the coach would overturn, I jumped down with my trunk, for if I had remained seated, zounds, how I likewise would have lain with my nose in the mud. Now I had to stifle my laughter at seeing the passengers wallow about in the muck. Now the postillion didn't know for the life of him how he would get out, because all four wheels of the coach were broken asunder. Perceiving now that there was no remedy at all for the coach, and knowing that I couldn't long delay, because I would see the city of Venice as soon as possible, I was quick to take my big trunk, thank my traveling companions, who still lay in the muck, for their company, and proceeded *per pedes* in the direction of Italy and France. That same day I wandered twenty-two miles on foot, and towards evening, with the setting sun, I came to a monastery wherein were the Brothers of Mercy, good fellows; the devil take me, they treated me right princely with foodstuffs, however they had no good beer in this monastery. I likewise asked them how it came that they had no good table drink; they answered me, they could not brew good beer because they had nothing but sour water. Whereupon I taught them a trick of brewing good sticky beer which would likewise taste so good that they would even sop it up with their fingers, and that they thereupon would learn how to preach excellently. Zounds! How the Brothers of Mercy thanked me for my trick which I had taught them. That same evening still they ran a sample; early the next morning, the devil take me, they had the finest sticky beer in a vat, tasting like pure sugar. Zounds, how the Brothers of Mercy drank to one another with sticky beer, they could hardly get enough, it tasted so good to them; soon they had to keep holding their mouths shut with their fingers, so avidly did they drink it down, and they weren't even aware of its going to their heads. The devil take me, I'll not my life long forget how good these fellows were to me on this account and how they honored me. Likewise they bade me stay a while with them, however I had no desire therefore. As I was now taking leave of them, they gave me a heap of victuals for the journey, that I should not starve; for just the day before (which was Friday in the monastery) the Brothers of Mercy had slaughtered six acorn swine, from which I got a long sausage and a tremendous piece of thick bacon for my trip. Now, the devil take me, I may say that my life long I had never seen bacon in the world such as I encountered there with the Brothers of Mercy, and if it wasn't six yards thick, then, the devil take me, I'm no fine fellow. Having now taken leave of the Brothers of Mercy, and larded my big trunk pretty well with provisions, I continued on my way to Venice. En route I overtook a fast post which was likewise of a will to drive to Venice, and because the postillion hadn't loaded many persons, I engaged the coach; yet I didn't trust myself to sit among the passengers for fear the post hand might likewise overturn like the previous one; and you couldn't know how an overturning might turn out, so I again sat in back on the luggage rack with my big trunk and bade the postillion drive on to Italy and France *per postae*. For some days we traveled very happily, and when we were about a gun shot from Venice, where you had to drive among big, hanging mountains, before we were aware of it, the postillion tipped over the post coach so that it toppled down one hill with us over a thousand times I suppose and, the devil take me, no one suffered the slightest injury. Except two wheels of the post coach, they went to the dogs. However those of us who were seated in the post coach were all covered with heavy sand dust, for around Venice there are nothing but sandy mountains. Likewise a heap of dust and sand had got into my big trunk, so that on the bacon which the Brothers of Mercy had given me, yard-thick sand and dust were lying. Perceiving now that the postillion would tarry long for lack of the two wheels on his post coach, I walked completely on foot to the city of Venice. However, the way the wind blew my eyes so full of sand and dust en route is, the devil take me, indescribable, for there was at that time an unheard of great wind. Yet I must admit that from the distance, the devil take me, the city of Venice presents itself right *propre*, for it is situated on a big, high, stony rock and is surrounded by an excellent wall. Having now reach-

ed the city of Venice on foot with my big trunk, I put up at the
White Ram where I had very good comfort and service. The
landlady, a widow, received me in a very friendly manner and
forthwith conducted me into a beautiful chamber wherein stood
over two hundred made up beds; this chamber she assigned me
for the custody of my belongings, and again took leave with a
polite *compliment*. Now alone in the beautiful chamber, I took
the trunk from my neck, opened it up, and took therefrom a
white shirt, for the shirt which I had worn very long on my
body, well, there was not exactly security therein, since I had
been presented with several regiments of boarders at the Brothers of Mercy. Now as soon as I had got these from my body and
had put on a white shirt, I hid my big trunk with my things
under a made up, pretty bed, so that no one should find it, and
again stepped out of the chamber, locked it up, and asked the
landlady what was new and interesting in Venice. Answering
me, the landlady said there were all sorts of interesting things
(since it was fair time) to see in St. Mark's Square. Zounds,
how I turned toward St. Mark's Square when the landlady chattered of a fair. Forthwith I was quick to fetch the big trunk
again with my things from my room. I hung it on me so that it
might not in any way get away from me since it was fair time.
When I now came to St. Mark's Square, zounds, what beautiful
houses stood there, the like of which I had never yet seen in Holland, England, nor in Sweden, nor all India, nor anywhere. The
devil take me, they were adorned with the costliest pieces of
marble, one house was I suppose over fifty stories high, and in
front of each house round about the marketplace stood a great
pump for the reason that water is so rare there. Now in the center of St. Mark's Square stood a big booth of fortune. Now any-
body who would, grabbed therein, but the person had to pay a
ducat for each grab, however there were likewise winnings
therein of sixty thousand to seventy thousand thalers. Likewise
there were also very low winnings, for the lowest winning was
worth only about one farthing, which makes six pennies in
Germany.

Perceiving now that many people were winning nicely, I
was quick likewise to risk a ducat thereon and would try my luck.
When I now reached into the pot of fortune, zounds, how many
slips of paper were there, I'll wager there were well over one
thousand million shocks of slips of paper present in the pot of

fortune. Now feeling into the pot of fortune with both hands, I made such a grab that I almost should have pulled out all the slips at once with both fists. Noticing this, zounds, how the pot of fortune man rapped my fingers for pulling out so many slips; and I had to throw them all back in again forthwith, and thereupon take out only a single slip for my ducat, which I likewise did. Having now for my ducat drawn a slip out of the pot of fortune and opened it (it was a good number and indeed number eleven), I was now obliged to show this to the man at the booth of fortune. Now everybody thought I should get something big therefrom, because I had snagged an odd number. When however it was revealed what number eleven signified, it turned out to be a little beard brush worth about six pennies. Zounds! How all the people standing about the booth laughed at me with my little beard brush. However I payed no attention at all, but was quick to reach into the pot of luck again, pulling out another slip which again had a good number, for it was number 0983726-41509. Zounds! How all the people in and around the booth of fortune gaped with their mouths that I had seized such an excellent number. Now I suppose that the heart of the booth man must have told him forthwith that I had seized something really good from his booth, for just as soon as the slip was visible, he began to sweat terribly, and it reeked about him as though he had scented his trousers inclusively and exclusively with a strong fragrance.

When they now checked in the booth of fortune to determine the winning of my excellent number, it turned out to be a horse of five hundred reichthalers, and the wife of the booth man, who was tabbed at one thousand ducats. Oh, *morbleu!* What a crowding when it became known that Signor Schelmuffsky had done so well in the booth of fortune. Forthwith I was obliged to mount the horse which I had won, and the thousand ducats won in place of the booth man's wife were all strung on a chaplet; I was obliged to hang this around my big trunk and ride about the whole city that the people might see my prizes. Ninety-nine drummers, ninety-eight shawmers, three lute players, and one zither player had to precede my horse; the two lutes and the sole zither sounded likewise so charming among the drums and shawms that, the devil take me, you couldn't hear your own words. During this however I sat on my horse very nicely. I suppose the horse must

have been trained at a riding school and dance hall, for it danced
in time with the music and, the devil take me, stepped along with
an incomparably stately gait. The devil take me, I can't describe
adequately how the women stared at me as I approached St.
Mark's Square, for they were laughing at my whole appearance
and everyone could quickly count on his fingers that the like of
me would indeed be pretty difficult to find in the world.

During this riding about I suppose over thirty persons of
nobility sent to me on the street to express their most humble
greetings and bade me politely inform them who I was and of
what position so that they might be enabled to pay calls which
were highly due me. However I had these persons of nobility
very nicely informed by way of reply that as a matter of fact I
had indeed tried something of note in the world and had been
in Sweden, Holland, and England; likewise I had spent fourteen
whole days at the Great Mogul's in India where at his excellent
castle in Agra I had experienced much honor; now who I should
be they could easily deduce. Hereupon I now rode forth again
with my music, and when I would parade before the town hall,
twenty-six bailiffs unexpectedly grabbed the bridle of my horse
and all screamed in chorus: "Halt." As I was now obliged to
stop, the great members of the council consisting of fourteen
hundred nobles stepped up, bowed to me, and considered themselves fortunate to have the high honor of enjoying my aristocratic presence. Having now returned their compliments, I answered quite nicely on horseback half in the English, half Dutch,
as well as occasionally in the German language too.

Now no sooner was my speech of reply finished, than all the
councilors bade me dismount and be their esteemed guest. Whereupon I forthwith dismounted with my big trunk and ordered my
horse led to the bailiffs' quarters until I had eaten, which order
was executed. Three presidents therewith conducted me in the
middle up to the town hall, all the members of the council were
now walking behind me all in files of one dozen. Ascending now
eleven stairs in the town hall, oh zounds! What a beautiful hall
was there revealed. It was exclusively plastered with polished
works of glass art and in place of panelling, the walls were en-
tirely adorned with marble stucco which almost blinded your
eyes. In the middle of the hall, not far from the stairs, stood a
long, set table carved of Venetian glass whereon the rarest and

most delicate foods were placed. With my big trunk I was now
obliged to sit quite at the head of the table, and beside me sat the
three presidents who had conducted me up the eleven stairs.
Farther down the table sat the other members of the council,
and all observed me with the greatest astonishment that I had
such an appetite for eating. Now during the course of the meal
all sorts of things were discoursed about; however I sat initially
quite still and acted as if I couldn't count to three. Having however sated myself, I thereupon opened up my mouth too and began to relate how I once had been given such excellent gifts in
India by the Great Mogul, how I had to keep account of his income for him, how I had turned up half as much surplus as he
took in annually, and how therefore the Great Mogul would make
me his chancellor of the realm because I understood Adam Riese's
arithmetic book so well. Zounds! How the gentlemen of the
council at Venice listened as I chattered about the chancellor of
the realm and Adam Riese's arithmetic book. Hereafter they titl-
ed me exclusively Your Reverence and all began forthwith to
toast my health. First one said: "Long live that person who
could have become chancellor of the realm of the Great Mogul
but who declined to accept." Soon another began with: "Long
live he who can turn up half as much surplus above the Great
Mogul's income, even though it is not his duty to collect it."
These and similar toasts were now being proposed in my honor
by all around the glass table. My health having now made the
rounds, the one president sitting hard by turned to me with the
remark that I should not after all keep my high birth secret any
longer, for from my discourses he had perceived that I must not
be of poor origin, but rather something uncommon was shining
out of my eyes. Whereupon I considered whether or not I would
reveal my identity. Finally I thought, defecation, you only want
to relate the incident of the rat to them that they will be obliged
to open up their mouths and ears big for sheer pleasure. And I
was quick to begin to chatter about the rat and the kind of hole
it had run into. Zounds! What a great sensation this thing caused with the fourteen hundred councilors when I began to chatter about the rat. The devil take me, they all put their heads
together at the table and talked furtively about me for I suppose
three whole clock hours; however I couldn't understand a word
of what they were whispering to one another. Yet as much as
I could gather from my neighbor to the right, he was saying to

one president, that if I would accept, I could become superinten-
dent of the Venetian council, since otherwise they had no one
suitable for this. Having now all thus secretly consulted one
another, they all began to speak at once, saying: "We would
make Your Reverence overseer of the council, we hope you will
accept?" Replying to this very good offer, I forthwith said to the
entire town council very nicely:

"Much honored gentlemen and esteemed bosom friends, now
the fact that I am a fine fellow is not to be questioned, and that
I have tried my hand at something important in the world at sea
as well as on land, the famous pirate Hans Barth himself will
have to admit, from whose crooked hawk's nose I sabered off a
big chunk with my excellent back scratcher. In short, the
like of me and my deportment will scarcely be found in the
world." Zounds! How the fourteen hundred councilors all gazed
at me upon hearing of my back scratcher and my deportment.

Whereupon one president likewise said to me forthwith,
that the entire council had now gathered from my answer that I
should hardly accept the proffered *charge*, since my disposition
was only inclined to traveling. To which I now kept quiet as a
mouse, made an extraordinarily nice *compliment* to the three
presidents, and, before they were aware of it, I stood up from
the table like a flash of lightning. Now noticing that I was getting up, they too all began to arise together.

Now having observed that I would not tarry with them any
longer, the entire council presented me an artfully cut Venetian
glass valued at twenty thousand thalers which I should keep in
eternal memory of them and occasionally toast their health from
it. It should have happened thusly too if I had not unexpectedly
broken it to pieces, as you will hear later.

Having now again taken leave of the entire Venetian council
and thanked for the great honor shown me, I stuck the beautiful,
costly glass presented me into my big trunk and had several
bailiffs again bring up from the bailiffs' quarters my horse won
in the booth of fortune to the hall upstairs. There I now again
mounted my horse with my trunk and rode down the stairs in
full course with such a nice *manière* that all the councilors were
highly amazed at my riding and surely thought I should break
my neck and legs because it was so slick on the stairs,
the steps being made of the most beautiful, cut Venetian glass;
however my horse was adept, not even slipping, it trotted down

the glass stairs with me like a flash of lightning. Down there
before the bailiffs' quarters my musicians were now watching
for me again, and as soon as they saw me come riding down from
the town hall, they forthwith struck up a saraband with their
trumpets, but the shawmers piped the dance of death therein,
and the two with the lutes played the song: "I've not been with
you for so long," and the man with the zither strummed the Old-
enburg Peasant Dance in the rear.

Well, the devil take me, I can't say how excellently the music
sounded, and to this my horse kept making one hop and skip
after another. Now I would once more therewith ride around St.
Mark's Square only thereby to lure people to the windows that
they might be soundly astonished at my excellent riding, which
result happened too. For as I again came riding across St. Mark's
Square with my big trunk, I suppose well on to thirty thousand
people stuck their heads out the windows; they almost went crazy
over me because I sat on my horse so *galant* with my big trunk.
I was so delighted with this business of the people staring so
stoutly at my excellent posture on horseback that, the devil take
me, I shall never forget it my life long. But the fie which I con-
tributed in this same connection, of this the little Venetian street
lads can still chatter to this day.

Just hear how it came about. While I was now riding quite
nicely about St. Mark's Square with my big trunk and all the
people were opening up their mouths and noses at me, I pulled
a pistol out of one holster and fired therewith. But the man at
the booth of fortune had not told me previously (when I had won
the horse at his booth) that it was gunshy and should smell no
powder. As now in all splendor I shot off the pistol, the horse
lurched before I realized it and, the devil take me, hurled me
forthwith out of the saddle with my big trunk so that I fell flat
on my face on St. Mark's Square, and the beautiful glass which
was so costly broke into one hundred thousand pieces. Zounds!
How all the people began to laugh at me. But I was quick to get
up again quickly and kept running after the horse and would
fain catch it again; now when I was close to it, and would seize
the gallows bird from behind by its tail, the miserable jade repeatedly began to dance and prance rapidly up one street, down
the other. I chased the old nag I suppose three whole hours around
the city of Venice and still couldn't catch it. Finally it even ran
out through the city gate into a patch of oats sewn hard by the

gate on a stony rock. Well, I thought now, I would snatch it, and
kept running after it in the oats, but, the devil take me, I could-
n't catch hold of it, for the more I chased after the carrion, the
farther it trotted into the field, luring me with its tomfoolery up
to the city of Padua before I could get it again. I think I should
hardly have caught it yet if a peasant had not come driving out
of the city of Padua with a manure wagon, he had a mare hitched
to his wagon; the horse which I had won stopped still (because
it was a stallion) beside the mare.

Now that I had it again, I forthwith remounted with my
big trunk and conferred there with my thoughts whether I would
again ride forthwith into Venice or into the city of Padua posthaste to see same. Soon I thought in my mind, where after all will
the musicians think forever and eternally that Signor Schelmuffsky has gone with his big trunk, since he is not returning?
Again, I likewise thought, if you ride back to Venice and come
to St. Mark's Square, the people again will look at von Schelmuffsky heartily and the small lads will whisper into one anoth-
ers' ears: "'Hey, look, there comes the aristocratic gentleman
riding again with his trunk whom the horse threw down on the
street flat on his face four hours ago, let's really give him a good
laugh." Finally, I likewise thought, if you come back to Venice
and the council learns that you broke the beautiful glass to pieces, they'll present you the next time with a trifle. Whereupon I
made a quick resolution, thinking: "Good night, Venice, Signor
Schelmuffsky must see what things look like in Padua" whereupon I kept running into the city of Padua with a full pace.

# The Fourth Chapter

Padua is a fine city, the devil take me, though not very large, it has solely new houses and is situated a half hour from Rome. It is very populous with students because such a stout university is there. Occasionally there are over thirty thousand students in Padua who are all made doctors in one year. For, the devil take me, you can easily become a doctor there if you just have bacon in your pocket and aren't afraid to speak up. I put up in said city with my horse and big trunk in an inn (called At the Sign of the Red Bull) where there was a valiant, imposing landlady. Well, as soon as I dismounted from the horse with my big trunk, the landlady forthwith came running out to me, fell upon my neck and kissed me, however she was convinced I was her son. For she too had sent a son abroad and because unannounced I now came riding fast into her courtyard and she saw me only from behind, she might well believe her son was coming riding, so she immediately came reeling toward me, grabbed me by the back of my head and embraced me. However after I told her that I was so and so and had likewise rummaged everywhere about the world, she thereupon begged my pardon for being so bold.

This same landlady also had several daughters, the devil take me, they conducted themselves *galamment* and *proprement* in their dress, only it was too bad that these females were so haughty and adept in finding fault with everyone, since, the devil take me, they themselves were to be criticized from top to bottom. For no one could walk by their house in peace whom they didn't always criticize, and they quarreled day after day with their mother. Indeed, at times they even bore down so hard on their mother that it was a sin and shame and they became so accustomed to ugly cursing and swearing that, the devil take me, I often thought: "What's this all about? The femaies will have to die on the manure pile yet because they curse their own mother so." However it served the mother quite right, why hadn't she reared them better in their youth. Also she still had a small son at home, he still was the best, she maintained various tutors for him, but this boy had no desire for studies. He found his sole pleasure in doves and likewise (like me in my youth) in the pea-shooter. When it was market day he always shot passing peasants on the head therewith, hereafter he hid behind the house door, that no one might see him. I felt inclined toward the boy merely on account of the pea-shooter, because I too had been such a fool about this in my youth.

Now there were likewise many students there in the house with whom the landlady's daughters were on excellent terms. Of a morning they always ran up to the students in their rooms and pestered them until they were obliged to order a good breakfast. Now whether the mother saw or knew that her daughters were visiting at the students' rooms, in any case, the devil take me, she didn't make the slightest remark, but when she noticed that the students had ordered a good glass of wine, she likewise joined in the business and drank with them until the glasses were empty. Hereupon she again went her way and told her daughters to come down soon when they had had enough, which they likewise did sometimes. However I could never stand the females around me, for in the first place they didn't speak a sensible word with you, and if you wanted to talk to me at that time, the devil take me, you had to be brazen. In the second place at once I had an aversion to these females, for whenever they came close to me, they had a miserable, foul-smelling breath.

Now I suppose the good girls couldn't help this, for as far as I could determine from the odor, they probably had acquired the defect from their mother, for the devil take me, you could smell her forthwith even though you didn't even see her. This landlady likewise would fain have a husband again, if only some man would have her, for that devilish bastard Cupid must have given her an atrocious, big wound with his arrow to cause her still at sixty to look so amorous about her mouth. I wager she could still have got a proposition (since she had a good income), but she stank so scandalously about her neck that whoever saw her even from afar forthwith lost all appetite. All day long she talked of nothing but matchmaking and her son who was abroad, saying what a stately fellow he was.

I don't believe I had lodged at this landlady's quite three weeks before her son from abroad turned up at home again. The devil take me, he showed up like a tinker and stank of tobacco and brandy like the worst marauder. Zounds! How this fellow bragged about where he had been, pure lies, the devil take me.

Now after his mother and sisters, as well as his little brother had welcomed him, he would begin to speak French with his sisters, but, the devil take me, he couldn't produce anything but *"Oui."* When they then asked him in German whether he likewise had been here or there, he answered each time: *"Oui."* His little brother likewise began to speak to him, saying: "I've been told that you didn't get any farther than Halle in Saxony, can that be true?" For answer he replied *"oui"* to him too. When now he too answered with *"oui"* thereto, the devil take me, I was obliged to bite my tongue to prevent my laughter, that he might not notice that I understood these matters better than he. For I could see it forthwith in his eyes that he could not have been over a mile away from Padua. Since speaking French would not come very fluently for him, he began to speak German and would fain chatter with a foreign flavor. However his dear mother tongue kept exposing him so that even the smallest child could have noticed that his speaking with a foreign flavor was pure and forced affectation. I now acted quite naive thereby and at first didn't mention a word about my travels. Well, the fellow now came up with things which forthwith would have pained your ears, and not a single word was true. For I knew all this better because long before I had already worn down my shoes on these same lands and cities where he claimed to have been.

The students in the house called him exclusively The Foreigner on the grounds that he would have been everywhere. Just consider the horrible, big lies that this devilish fellow, The Foreigner, put forward; for when I asked him whether he had seen and endured anything important here and there at sea, he gave me such a long answer that I could make neither head nor tail of such slush. Zounds! How this business with the base sluggard vexed me, to think he was chattering such slush to me, it wouldn't have taken much for me to deal him a blow to make him stick forthwith to the corner of the table, however I thought: "Why bother, you will only cause him to exaggerate and get to hear what else he will shoot off about." Besides, The Foreigner now began to chatter about navigation. Now the devil take me, I can't say what a fuss the fellow made about ships and especially about those ships which one calls towboats. For he told his sisters in great astonishment how he had sailed on a towboat from Holland to England in one day with two thousand persons with terrible turbulence and sheet lightning and hadn't wet a shoe. Whereover The Foreigner's sisters were very astonished. Hereto however I uttered no word, but was obliged to have a right hearty inward laugh because The Foreigner was

making such a fuss there about the paltry towboat. Only I would
not scold him and answer his bragging. For if the fellow should
have heard how I had had to float on a plank with my dead
brother the count over a hundred miles before we could even
smell land and how likewise at that time a single plank had
saved the lives of fifty of us, zounds, how The Foreigner would
have popped open his ears and looked at me, however I thought.
you might as well let him brag, why are the females such fools
to be so quickly astonished at such slush. Further, The Foreigner
also related how he had been in London and had been so esteemed by the ladies that a very aristocratic lady had so fallen
in love with him that she couldn't live a day without him, for
if he did not come to her every day, she forthwith sent a valet
to him; he was always obliged to fetch him in a carriage drawn
by eleven yellow, black horses, and when he now had come to
this aristocratic lady, she first always arranged a good jag of
mastic water for him before beginning to chatter with him of
amorous matters.

He likewise claimed to have progressed so far with this
same lady that she payed him a daily fee of fifty thousand
pounds sterling that he might now begin only what he himself
would fain have done. Zounds! Again what lies from The
Foreigner, and his sisters, well, the devil take me, they believed
everything he said. One asked him how much a pound sterling
was worth in German coin anyway. He replied, a pound sterling
was six pennies in German coin. Oh, zounds! How this business
of this fellow vexed me, to think that he valued a pound sterling
at only six pennies, since after all a pound sterling in German
coin is a farthing which is worth half a lump in Padua. Nothing
caused me to laugh inwardly so heartily for myself than that
The Foreigner's little brother always interfered whenever The
Foreigner told lies, for he would not believe a single word at
all, but kept wondering how The Foreigner could take the trouble
of chattering about these and those countries in view of the
fact that after all he had not got over a mile from Padua. This
business annoyed The Foreigner, however he would not say
much, because it was his brother, nevertheless he gave him this
answer: "Boy, you know a lot about horse trading." The little
brother was likewise irked by this business of The Foreigner's
calling him a boy and chattering about horse trading, for the
wicked little toad likewise imagined that he was already a big
fellow because he had been carrying a sword from his sixth into

his fifteenth year. He quickly ran to his mother and complained to her that his foreign brother had called him a boy. This likewise vexed the mother, she was quick to give him money and send him to the university in Padua that he might there matriculate and become a student.

When he now came back, he began to address his brother, saying: "Well, now I too have really become an upright fellow, I defy anyone to consider me otherwise." The Foreigner looked at his little brother from head to toe, from front to back, with a scornful countenance and, having observed him all over, said: "You still look boyish enough." This business vexed the little brother frightfully, to have The Foreigner scold him thusly before everyone. He was quick then to whip out his little blade and said to The Foreigner: "If you have something to criticize about me or if you opine that I am no upright fellow, then have a care for my sword, I'll show you what student manners are like." Now The Foreigner had very little heart in his body when he saw his little brother's small sword. He began to tremble and shake and for great anxiety couldn't say a word, until finally his little brother did sheathe his sword again and made up with The Foreigner. However, the devil take me, I can't tell how the new academician was heckled by the house boys and students. They called him only the green student, and when I asked wherefore they did this, I was answered, he was only called the green student because he wasn't yet very adept at the university, furthermore his mother hired a tutor for him daily who was obliged to teach him *Donatus* and *Grammatica*. However, that the green student would not have the shame as if he were still being taught by the rod, he pretended to the other students that the tutor was his roommate.

Now after one of the house boys had told me such and would tell me still more things about the green student I was forthwith summoned to the table.

Now at table The Stranger again began to brag about his travels and related how he had been in France and had by a hair just missed having the honor of seeing the king. His sisters now asking him about what the new styles were in France, he answered them that whoever would fain see the latest dress and styles should merely ask him, for up to the present he was still keeping his own tailor in France, to whom he payed annual retainers whether he made him anything or not; whoever would fain have something of the newest styles made by this tailor

should merely come to him (namely to The Foreigner). He
would send the order to the tailor, for this tailor dared not sew
a stitch for anyone else, if The Foreigner would not have it
so. The devil take me, I can't say how The Foreigner extolled
his personal tailor and thereby scorned all other tailors in the
whole world, especially would he have nothing at all to do with
the tailors in Germany, for these (opined The Foreigner)
weren't worth a shot of powder because they wasted so much.
After he had related this, and his maiden sisters fain would
not say much hereto, he called the house boy, who was obliged
to run quickly to the apothecary's and fetch him four groschen
of mastic water. Now, the devil take me, I can't tell the fuss
and boasting The Foreigner made about the mastic water; how
as a matter of fact the same was so healthful for morning sickness in the early morning, likewise for earache, and how it could
rake your stomach so solidly back in shape if your throat felt
like vomiting. However I thought in my mind, you just keep
on extolling your mastic water, I shall stick to my olive oil. For
I say it once more, when you feel ill, there is nothing more
healthful or better in the world than a good little glass full of
olive oil. When now the house boy came with the mastic water,
zounds, how The Foreigner drank the stuff into him greedily; it
was just as if he were pouring a glass of water into him, and
his eyes didn't even water therefrom.

The Foreigner now having taken mastic water to heart for
four groschen, he began further to relate concerning business
and commerce in Germany, and told how most merchants didn't
really understand their business and how not even one merchant
in a hundred knew what commerce was. In France on the other
hand there were fine merchants, they knew much more about
business than the stupid Germans. Zounds! How I listened as
The Foreigner chattered about the stupid Germans. Now since
I was German from birth, the devil take me, I should have acted
as the worst sluggard if I had kept quiet thereto; however I
forthwith began saying to him: "Now listen, fellow! Why are
you abusing the Germans, I too am a German, and he's a cur
who doesn't estimate them as the finest people." I had hardly
rubbed the word cur under the nose of The Foreigner when he
gave me unexpectedly a blow that forthwith my chops swelled
up therefrom like a fried sausage. However I was quick to grab
The Foreigner behind the table by his black crown in such a
nice *manière* and in return for the one blow I gave him I sup-

pose a thousand blows. Zounds, how his sisters, likewise the green student and the tutor, or, to say it rightly, the green student's roommate, got into my hair and really disheveled me. However I unraveled myself as fast as possible from the press, leaped from behind the table, ran toward the tile stove; there I had my big trunk hanging on a wooden nail in the warm spot behind the stove, I took this down and because it was right heavy with the bacon (which I had got presented from the Brothers of Mercy in the monastery), you could have seen nice trunk pounding there as I thoroughly pounded not only The Foreigner's sisters and the green student, but also the green student's tutor (oh, I would say roommate) and The Foreigner himself there. In great anxiety The Foreigner with perilous labor threw up the mastic water which he had drunk in so greedily at table and with continuous vomiting requested good weather so that, finished vomiting, he would settle the whole business with me by means of the blade.

Oh, zounds! What a joy for me to hear The Foreigner chatter about the blade, whereupon I forthwith said fine and no longer hit him with my big trunk. However I was pounding the green student's roommate most pitiably, and I say that finally I should certainly have pounded him to death if The Foreigner's mother and sisters had not pleaded so dreadfully for him, for he stood on extremely good terms with his sisters and mother. The mother, that is to say the landlady, often said to the other house boys that she had never before had such a fine person as a tutor for her son as she now had, and if he remained thus, he were worth framing in gold. But the others whom she had had previously had all mostly deceived her, she especially kept telling about one at the Sign of the White Head; he had borrowed so much money from her and had never once paid anything back again, and about one who could open all the locks and secretly stolen many things from her, however I have forgotten their names again.

Now after The Foreigner was finished vomiting again, I hung my big trunk in the warm spot behind the stove again, drew out my long rapier which I bore at that time and hereupon challenged him to step before the gate. The Foreigner also produced his sword, now this was a musketeer's sword with a horrible hilt, therewith we both now marched toward the gate posthaste. The green student likewise would come running after with his roommate, but I and The Foreigner chased the sluggards back again. As we now came out by the gate, there was forthwith a high, pointed mountain hard by the circular wall; we climbed up same and up there on the peak of the mountain we walked together. To be sure we could have fought below the mountain, but we had no seconds with us, for if we had had seconds, they would have been obliged to stand behind us with bare swords, that no one of us could give ground. Lacking same however the high, pointed mountain had to second us, for likewise no one of us two could yield, for if even one had moved a straw's breadth from his position, then, the devil take me, we all should have tumbled down the mountain and broken our necks and legs fragilely in two as a result of our brawl; thus however while exchanging blows I and The Foreigner were obliged to stand stiff as a wall on our legs up there on the peak. However, before we began to duel, The Foreigner addressed me, saying I should cut at him since he had no thrusting sword, or, if it pleased me, he would cut at me for the first round, the second round he would try thrusting at me. But now perceiving that The Foreigner had no heart, I nevertheless said: "Just look out, fellow, it's all the same to me. I won't make a long ceremony with you." Therewith we both drew and cut at each other. Oh, zounds! How I drew my rapier from the sheath in such a nice *manière*, but the first cut I delivered with my rapier at The Foreigner cut his big short sword smoothly away from its hilt, and in the withdrawal I used the high fourth position to graze his nose and, the devil take me, I chopped off from his head both ears for him. Oh, zounds! How The Foreigner wailed at seeing his ears lying before him. I was likewise of a will to give him a stub nose like the pirate Hans Barth's, but because he held the wounds so sorely and bade me leave him unharmed, his life long he would scorn no German again, but should always say that the Germans were the finest people under the sun, I therefore sheathed my rapier again and bade him take both ears and wander therewith to the barber as fast as possible, perhaps they could be healed onto him again.

Hereupon he was quick to wrap his ears in a handkerchief, put his split short sword together with the big basket hilt under his arm, and walked with me into the city of Padua. In the big house hard by the gate beside the watcher dwelt a famous surgeon who was likewise supposed to have traveled well. To him I bade The Foreigner go with his hewn off ears that he should see whether they might possibly be healed on to

him again. But The Foreigner had no desire to go to the surgeon, rather he said he would first pour out a good little glass
of mastic water onto his pains; later he would betake himself
to the knacker for treatment and hear from him whether his
ears could be healed on again. Having told me this, he left me,
continuing his march to the apothecary's. However I was quick
secretly to sneak into the house of The Foreigner's mother
(where I had my quarters) that no one should see me, and ex-
tracted my big trunk out of the room from the warm spot behind the stove in such a nice *manière,* remounted the horse which
I had won, and kept on riding there, without paying the stable
fee and without taking leave, out of the city of Padua towards
Rome. From that time on I did not see again with any eye The
Foreigner, nor the green student with his tutor, or I should
say, his roommate. However I later heard from the university
messenger from Padua that the knacker was said fortunately
to have healed on The Foreigner's ears again in two days. But
during the two days he had exercised diligence with him, and
during the course of the cure The Foreigner had drunk down
twelve tankards of mastic water completely alone and (opined
the university messenger) from same mastic water he had mostly been restored again.

As concerns the green student and tutor as well as the entire family of The Foreigner, to date I have been able to learn
nothing about what they must be doing.

Now, *adieu,* Padua, Signor Schelmuffsky must see what
Rome looks like.

# The Fifth Chapter

The devil take me, Rome is likewise a stout city, only it's forever and eternally a shame that it has no view from without. It is built in pure reed and sedge and is surrounded about by a water which is called the Tiber River, and the Tiber flows through the middle of Rome down past the market place. For no one can walk to the market place, rather, when it's market day there, the peasants are obliged to sell their butter and cheese or geese and poultry exclusively in towboats. Zounds! How countlessly numerous are the towboats to be seen daily on the Roman market place. No matter who would fain sell even half a set of fifteen eggs in Rome, he tows them into the market on a towboat so that likewise many a day there are several thousand towboats drawn up there among the rows of peasants and none can move for the other. There are always excellent fish to be had on market days in Rome, and especially as concerns herring, the devil take me, they are at once fat and gleaming like a bacon rind and are extremely good eating, especially if they are well basted with rich olive oil.

Now to be sure it is no wonder that there are such fat herrings there for, the devil take me, there is an extremely good herring fishery by Rome on the Tiber, and the city of Rome is celebrated far and wide in the world on account of its herring. No matter where your woman selling herring is located in Germany, and no matter how many herring she has or would fain have, the devil take me, they're all caught on the Tiber by Rome, for the herring fishery belongs to the Pope, and because his feet are not always well and he himself can wait, he has leased the herring fishery to several seamen; they must pay the Pope a large annual tribute therefrom.

Now coming riding up to Rome with my big trunk to horse, I could not ride into the city of Rome on account of the Tiber, but rather was obliged to embark on a towboat with my big trunk and horse and be shipped into the city of Rome.

Having now arrived safely on the towboat with my big trunk to horse, I took quarters with a stargazer who dwelt on Herring Street, not far from the Delicacies Market. The devil take me, he was an extremely fine man and celebrated almost in the entire world on account of his star gazing. Especially as concerns the fixed stars, therefrom he could prophesy frightening things, for whenever it was raining merely a little and the sun had hidden behind turbid clouds, he could tell you forthwith that the sky was not very clear. Now this very stargazer led me around the entire city of Rome and showed me all the antiquities to be seen there so that I saw so much from such showing that I now cannot recall anything more thereof. Finally he likewise led me near St. Peter's Church into a large stone house covered with marble tiles, and when we entered therein and went up to a beautiful hall, there an old man in fur stockings sat in a grandfather's chair and slept; to him on order of the stargazer I was obliged to slip quietly, pull off his fur stockings, and thereafter kiss his feet.

Now the devil take me, I cannot tell how much the legs of the old fellow stank, I'll wager that he hadn't had them washed in a half year. Having now kissed his stinky legs, I would awaken him and ask why he didn't have a maid bring a tub of water every evening to wash his legs, since one was obliged to kiss his feet (since it was the *mode*) ; however the stargazer beckoned to me that I should not disturb his sleep, and told me quite softly that I should again put the fur stockings on His Holiness. Zounds! Hearing the word Holiness, how I hastened to put his fur stockings on his legs again, and marched down from the hall out of the house with the stargazer again. Now the stargazer told me indeed that it was the feet of His Papal Holiness which I had kissed and likewise opined that any foreign German coming to Rome and failing to kiss the feet of the Pope dare not later (after he returned to Germany) boast of having been in Rome if he had not done such.

And thus I can rightly say that I have been in Rome, unless it should turn out that the stargazer used the fixed star to pull some blue wool over my eyes and that it was maybe an old errand boy whose legs had stunk so much. However if I should swear that it was certainly the Pope whose feet I had kissed, then, the devil take me, I could not do this in good conscience, for the stargazer appeared to me as if he were capable of skulduggery because he had his heart so set on the fixed star; no sooner did he think of the fixed star than he knew right away what kind of weather was predicted in the calendar.

This same stargazer was an excellent calendar maker, he likewise taught me the same art, I have made very many calendars too, they are all completed and lying under the bench, yet, the devil take me, occasionally they still come pretty much true. If I should hear that there are connoisseurs thereof, I should mayhap pull one out sometime and publish it as a sample. Yet time brings counsel.

However to return to my previous theme of relating whither else the stargazer conducted me after I had kissed the feet of the Pope. Hard by St. Peter's Church was a quite narrow little street, the stargazer kept leading me through this up to the market place. Having now arrived at the market place he asked me whether I should fain board a towboat to take a little ride along to the herring fishery. Wherewith I forthwith agreed. Thereupon we both seated ourselves in a towboat and, having a favorable wind, we kept sailing on the Tiber past the market down toward the herring gate through a drain.

Arriving now at the herring fishery with our towboat, zounds, what wailing from the seamen who had leased the herring fishery. When I now asked what the trouble was, they told me with crying eyes how Barth the pirate with the stub nose had caused them great injury in their sustenance and had, with other pirates, roguishly stolen over forty tuns of fresh herring from them only a half of a quarter hour ago. Zounds, how wrathful I was to hear of Hans Barth's stub nose; I thought forthwith, it must be the same fellow who once on the Spanish Sea with terribly many pirates had arrested me without *raison* and had therewith made me a poor man. Whereupon I was quick to question the sailors whither the rogue had marched with the tuns of herring. As they now told and showed me that he could still be seen on the Tiber with his pirate ship whereon he had packed the forty tuns of fresh herring, I quickly set out after him with several towboats, and because there was such an admirably good wind, I together with the stargazer and several sailors got hold of him a half mile from the herring fishery.

Zounds! How Hans Barth's heart dropped down to his britches when he only saw me coming from a distance; he became as red in the face as a piece of cheese and probably forthwith well recalled that I was so and so who previously had hung such a dreadful blemish on his nose. When in our towboats we now had caught up with Hans Barth and his forty stolen tuns of herring, I forthwith addressed him: "Now listen, fellow, will you give back the herring which you stole from the poor sailors or do you prefer that I should saber off completely your crooked stub hawk's nose? Whereupon answering me, Hans Barth said he would rather give up his life than give back peacefully even one tail of a herring. Hereupon I moved up to his pirate ship

with my towboat, got out my long, little sword; well, there you
could have seen some beautiful brandishing as I drilled Hans
Barth on his pirate ship; to be sure he and his pirates defended
themselves, however they couldn't do a thing to me. For even
though they hewed and stuck at me, I moved about securely
with my towboat like lightning; But Hans Barth I kept chasing
around the forty tuns of herring which he had loaded onto his
ship, the devil take me, and I hewed in at him higgledy-piggledy.
Finally I was so very vexed at the rascally bird, that I approached his pirate ship quite close with my towboat and, before
he realized it, grabbed hold of his thievish plumage, yanked
him off the pirate ship, and bluntly dipped him into the Tiber.
Zounds! You should have heard some nice screaming there by
Hans Barth; he begged me, almost for Heaven's sake, to help
him out again that he might not drown, he would gladly and
cordially give the forty tuns of herring back to the sailors.
Hearing this from Hans Barth, I ordered the sailors to plunder
the pirate ship and held him so long in the water by the ears
until they had their tuns of herring back again, whereupon I
let him sail with his empty pirate ship whither he would;
zounds, what a cry of jubilation arose from the seamen who
had leased the herring fishery because through me they had
again got their tuns of herring. Also, all together they implored
me to become their guardian of herring, they would pay me
ten thousand pounds sterling annually, however I had no in-
clination thereto. When now we again had arrived at the herring
fishery with our towboats and forty tuns of herring, the herring
leaseholders honored me with a tun of the best herring as a gra-
tuity; I loaded these onto my towboat and sailed therewith
along with the stargazer again into the city of Rome. Having
now come to the stargazer's quarters, I knocked open the tun
and tested a herring for taste. Now, the devil take me, I can no
longer say how fat these same herring were, that you couldn't
even devour without salt (since after all they had already been
heavily salted when they were put down). Now because I knew
that my Mother was a great lover of fresh herring, I packed
the presented tun of herring in my trunk and sent same to her
by a special messenger to Schelmerode in Germany, whereto I
likewise wrote her a very nice letter which was of the following
content:

With good and dear wishes foremost,
Respectable and honorable Mother,

If you are still in fine health and fettle, the devil take me, I
shall be really pleasured; I for the most part have again become
a fine fellow living in Rome where I have lodgings with a
stargazer who has taught me calendar making. You will likewise receive by this messenger fresh herring in my big trunk
which were presented me by the herring leaseholders of Rome.
As for the rest, the messenger will give you an oral report concerning my complete condition; I hope all goes well with you,
send me back a little cask of good sticky beer in my big trunk
and write me how you are and whether you still have the little
cousin with you, and I shall remain forever my respectable and
honorable Mother's

Ever most travel-desirous, sole, dear son,
Signor von Schelmuffsky
Rome, the first of April, in the year 090 after the building of
the City of Rome.

I now sent this letter together with my trunk full of fresh
herring to my Mother in Germany by a special messenger on
foot; fourteen days did not elapse before the messenger again
brought me the following in my big trunk by way of answer
from my Mother.

Respectable and renowned Bachelor von
Schelmuffsky, my dear Son.
I received your big trunk with the fresh herring and also read
your letter, and the messenger likewise told me your complete
condition whereof I was very pleased; as far as I am concerned,
I am presently sick to death, and if you will fain see me again,
come home forthwith; your little cousin sends his greetings, and
your maiden aunts wish you a good-day and likewise request
that you do come home forthwith. Farewell and don't stay too
long abroad, for my part I remain lifelong
Your dear Mother
Dwelling and resident in Germany
at Schelmerode.
Schelmerode the first of January 1621.
P. S. The sticky beer is presently all sour, otherwise I should
have been cordially happy to send you some.

When I had now read my Mother's letter, zounds, how I
packed everything together in my big trunk, saddled my horse,
took leave of the stargazer, again boarded a towboat with my

horse in the public square in the city of Rome and then kept on sailing down *per postae* past the herring gate out through a postern gate. Before the gate I got off the towboat, mounted my horse with my big trunk and kept on riding toward Germany. I made my way through Poland and rode towards Nürnberg where I lodged over night in the Golden Goose. From there I would fain make my way through the Black Forest which lies two miles away from Nürnberg. Hardly had I ridden a musket shot into the Black Forest before two robbers unexpectedly were on my neck; the devil take me, they took off all my clothes and chased me away in my bare shirt with a back full of blows. Zounds! How did I then feel, that my horse, my clothes, my thousand ducats, and my big trunk with all kinds of goods and chattels were gone.

Well, the devil take me, I could only grin and bear it. However there was nothing to do but see how I might find my way out of the Black Forest. And from there I conveniently begged all the way to Schelmerode. How I now in a bare shirt was welcomed at the home of my sick Mother and how my little cousin derided me, the same likewise can be read in the future very nicely either in the third part of my dangerous travel account or in my Curious Months whereof I made mention in the preface; wherefore everyone may then now speak with me:

Schelmuffsky's second part of his dangerous
travel account is now likewise
ended.